Stacey and the Mystery at the Empty House

Other books by
Ann M. Martin

Rachel Parker, Kindergarten Show-off
Eleven Kids, One Summer
Ma and Pa Dracula
Yours Turly, Shirley
Ten Kids, No Pets
Slam Book
Just a Summer Romance
Missing Since Monday
With You and Without You
Me and Katie (the Pest)
Stage Fright
Inside Out
Bummer Summer

BABY-SITTERS LITTLE SISTER series
THE BABY-SITTERS CLUB mysteries
THE BABY-SITTERS CLUB series

Stacey and the Mystery at the Empty House

Ann M. Martin

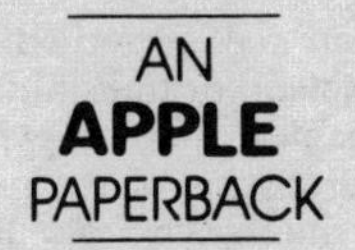

SCHOLASTIC INC.
New York Toronto London Auckland Sydney

If you purchased this book without a cover, you should be aware that this book is stolen property. It was reported as "unsold and destroyed" to the publisher, and neither the author nor the publisher has received any payment for this "stripped book."

ISBN 0-590-48233-5

12 11 10 9 8 7 6 5 4 3 2 1 4 5 6 7 8 9/9

Printed in the U.S.A. 40

First Scholastic printing, December 1994

The author gratefully acknowledges
Ellen Miles
for her help in
preparing this manuscript.

Stacey and the Mystery at the Empty House

"Ah, Paris!" said my mother. Suddenly, she got this faraway look in her eyes. *"Je n'ai jamais oublié Paris."*

"Mom, I never knew you spoke French," I said. "What does that *mean*?"

"It means 'I've never forgotten Paris,' " she said dreamily.

"Never forgotten?" I asked. "I didn't even know you'd ever *been* to France!"

"Oh, I've been there," she said softly. "I went to Paris for junior year abroad when I was in college. It was one of the most wonderful times of my life." She wrapped her arms around her shoulders and gave herself a little hug. "I even fell in love," she said softly.

"Fell in *love*?"

"Fell in love," she repeated. "His name was Jean-Paul, and his father was a famous chef. I almost married him and stayed in Paris." My mother still looked dreamy, as if she were off in another world. I'm sure she didn't notice how stunned I was. My mouth was hanging open so wide I felt as if my jaw were about to hit the floor.

"That's awesome." I said. "What happened?"

"Oh, my mother wouldn't have it," she answered. "As soon as she got wind of the idea she flew over and brought me back home." She sighed. "I'll always remember Jean-Paul," she said.

Whoa! My head was spinning. In the last three minutes I'd learned three new things about my mom:

1) She knew how to speak French. (Fluently, from what I could tell.)

2) She had lived in Paris. (Paris!)

3) (This one is major.) She had almost married a French guy.

It was number three that was really getting to me. It wasn't just that I was having a hard time imagining my mom in Paris, young and in love. I was, but that wasn't what was weirding me out. It was this: Suddenly I was realizing that my existence was only a matter of luck. I mean, what if she *had* married this Jean-Paul? I, Anastasia Elizabeth McGill (call me Stacey, *please*!), thirteen-year-old daughter of Edward and Maureen McGill, would not exist.

Or maybe I would exist in another form.

Maybe I'd be the *French* Stacey, daughter of Maureen and *Jean-Paul*. I'd be *très* sophisticated, used to dressing in Chanel and sipping coffee at cafes. I pictured myself in a little black suit —

"When are they leaving?" my mother asked.

The image of the French Stacey vanished. "What?" I asked. "Who? Leaving?" I must have sounded like somebody waking up from a dream, which in a way, I was.

"The Johanssens," said my mother. "When do they leave for France?"

"Oh, the *Johanssens*," I said, nodding. Of course. That was what had started this discussion. I'd been telling my mom about this extremely exciting thing that had happened to a girl I baby-sit for.

Her name's Charlotte Johanssen, and she's a favorite of mine. The Johanssens are regular clients of the BSC, which is this club I belong to, otherwise known as the Baby-sitters Club. I'll explain more about it later. Anyway, Charlotte's eight, and she and I are very close; in fact, we think of each other as "almost sisters." (I'm an only child, and so is she.) She's smart — she skipped a grade not long ago — and pretty (with big dark eyes, chestnut hair, and dimples), and a little shy. She used to be a *lot* shy, but I think I've helped her grow out of that.

Anyway, Charlotte's mom, who is a doctor, had just called me to tell me the news: Charlotte's Aunt Nell (her mom's older sister), who is an incredibly wealthy and successful art dealer, was planning a two-week tour of France in search of new artists. And, just for the heck of it, she'd invited her sister's family along for the ride! The Johanssens had accepted, and were taking Charlotte out of school so she could go, too.

When Dr. Johanssen finished telling me this, she asked if I might be willing to do her a favor. For a heart-pounding millisecond, I thought she was going to ask me to come along on the trip as a mother's helper.

No such luck. My assignment was much less glamorous.

Dr. Johanssen wanted to ask me if I'd walk Carrot, the family dog, twice a day. She also wanted me to keep an eye on the house. So instead of eating *croissants* in the shadow of the Eiffel Tower, I was going to be house-sitting and dog-walking for the next two weeks.

"They're leaving in two days," I said, answering my mother's question. "Can you believe it?"

"Charlotte must be so excited," said my mom.

"Oh, she is! At least, according to Dr. Johanssen. I haven't talked to her yet, but I'll see her in a little while. I'm going to sit for her today while the Johanssens take care of some last minute details for their trip."

"Passports," said my mom, getting that dreamy look again. "Luggage. Airline reservations . . . Oh, I *do* love to travel. I envy the Johanssens so much."

I looked at my mom with new understanding. This woman wasn't just a divorced mom, working as a buyer at a small-town department store and bringing up her daughter. Somewhere inside her was a free spirit, who could be living in France with a romantic, dark-haired (that was how I imagined him) French husband named Jean-Paul.

"Mom?" I asked. "Are you ever sorry you didn't marry that guy?"

"Who — Jean Paul?" She shook her head. "How could I be, honey? If I had, I wouldn't have you in my life now." She gave me a big hug.

I didn't mention my theory about the French Stacey. It seemed too complicated — and too silly — to go into. Instead, I just hugged my mother back.

She and I are very close. I guess that's partly because of my being an only child, and partly because of the divorce. I'm close to my dad, too, but I don't spend nearly as much time with him, since Mom and I live in Stoney-brook, Connecticut, and he lives in Manhattan.

That's where I grew up: New York, New York. "The city so nice they named it twice," as my dad used to say. I was a real city kid. As a baby I fell asleep to the sounds of traffic and fire engine sirens. When I was a toddler, I learned to climb stairs on the stoop outside our apartment house. By the time I was eight, I had been to the opera, could tell a Monet from a Picasso, and had seen *The Nutcracker* four times. By age ten, I knew how to nego-tiate the subways as well as most adults. And at twelve, I was buying all my own clothes.

Clothes. They've always been very impor-tant to me. Maybe that's also a part of being a city kid: in New York, I think even little children are aware of style. I *never* wore boring old pastels and ruffly dresses. My outfits were more like miniature versions of the latest fash-ions for adults. And now that I'm nearly an adult myself, I *still* seek out the coolest, most trendy clothes to wear.

Dressing the way I do has given me a certain reputation in Stoneybrook. I think most of the kids I go to school with, at Stoneybrook Mid-dle School, think I'm very sophisticated. It's because of the way I wear my clothes, I guess, and the way I perm my long blonde hair. But as my friends in the BSC know, I'm really just the same as everybody else: it's just that the *wrapper* is a little different.

Actually, there *is* one thing about me that's different from most kids I know: I am a diabetic. That means I have diabetes, which is a lifetime disease. My body doesn't process sugars well, so I have to help it along by giving myself injections of insulin every day, and also by being very careful about what I eat. Sweets are out; they can make me really sick.

Being forbidden to eat sweets sounds like a total nightmare to my best friend, Claudia Kishi. She's the Junk Food Queen of Stoneybrook. I think she *lives* on candy bars, chips, and sugar-filled sodas. (Don't tell her parents, though. She's not supposed to eat all that junk food.)

I called Claudia that Sunday afternoon to tell her about the Johanssens' trip. "Oh, my lord!" she said. "France. Think of all the shopping opportunities!"

Claudia is Japanese-American, with silky black hair that flows like a waterfall and deep, dark almond-shaped eyes. She's truly beautiful. And she loves clothes as much as I do. She has a funky, artistic, offbeat style of dressing that matches her funky, artistic, offbeat personality. She may not excel at school, the way her older sister Janine-the-genius does, but Claud has her own talents. I expect to be seeing her artwork at the Museum of Modern Art in a matter of years.

"I've *always* wanted to go to Paris," Claudia continued. "You could spend *days* in the Louvre and never see all the art."

"I'm sure the Johanssens will be going there," I said. "They'll probably hit *all* the museums." I paused and checked my watch. "Claud, I'd better get going. They're expecting me in a few minutes."

About ten minutes later, I was at the Johanssens' front door. They live in a small white house, with a picket fence surrounding the yard, and latticework trim on the back and front porches. Even though Charlotte's mom is a doctor, it's not a fancy house. It's small and cozy, and I've always felt very comfortable there.

I had barely knocked on the door when Charlotte threw it open. "Bon-jore!"

"Hi," I said, a little mystified.

"That's what *I* said," said Charlotte. "Only I said it in French. Bon-jore!" She grinned and twirled around, as if she could hardly contain herself. "Can you *believe* we're going to France?" she asked.

"It's great," I said. "It's *more* than great. It's wonderful. But — um, could I come inside? It's a little chilly out here." It was early December, not exactly porch-sitting weather.

"Oh, of course!" said Charlotte, ushering me in. "Voolay voo lah-vey rue!"

"What does *that* mean?" I asked.

"I don't know!" admitted Charlotte gaily. "I made it up. It *sounds* good, though, doesn't it?"

I laughed. "I bet nobody will know you're an American," I said. Then I switched to a fake French accent. "Your accent is *perfect*, mademoiselle." I bent to kiss her hand.

Charlotte giggled. "Mercy buckets," she said. "That means thank you very much."

Just then, Dr. Johanssen came down the stairs. "Oh, Stacey," she said. "Thanks so much for coming on such short notice. There isn't much we can accomplish on a Sunday, but we need to start working on our list." She held up a piece of paper covered with scribbles. "There's so much to *do!*"

"I'm glad I can help," I said.

"Now, about Carrot," Dr. Johanssen began. "I've written up some instructions for his care, and we can talk about it today before you leave. Basically, he just needs to be walked and fed. If he really needs to relieve himself, he can always go out the dog door and into the fenced run in the backyard, so if you'll come twice a day, he should be fine."

"No problem," I said.

"Wee, wee," said Charlotte, giggling.

"That's what he'll do when you walk him. It also means 'yes, yes' in French."

Dr. Johanssen smiled down at her daughter. "You're getting silly, Charlotte," she said. Then she looked back at me. "As far as house-sitting, there isn't much to it. Just keep an eye on the place, and bring in our newspapers and mail. I wrote all that down, too. All the instructions will be posted on the refrigerator, along with our itinerary — a schedule of where we'll be each day."

"Fine," I said.

"And here's a key," she went on. "You can take this with you today."

"Great," I said. "Sounds like we're all set." I was actually looking forward to house-sitting. It would be a nice change of pace.

But my anticipation was nothing compared to Charlotte's. She was so excited about her trip that she could talk about nothing else all afternoon. I helped her pick out clothes to pack, showed her how to tie a scarf in the European style, and listened to her practice her "French." And when it was time to say good-bye, I gave her a big hug and wished her "bon voyage." I knew she was going to have a great time.

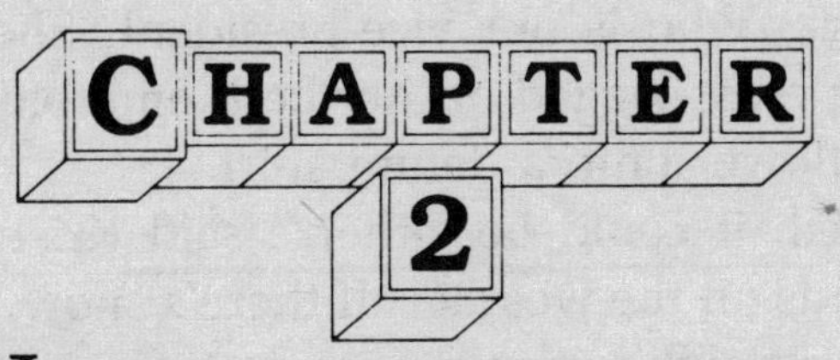

"Well, I know it isn't exactly a trip to *France,*" said Kristy, looking over at me and grinning. "But it does sound like it might be fun. And it's free, that's the best part. Let's think it over, at least."

It was 5:40 on Monday afternoon and the BSC was in the middle of a meeting. Seven of us were gathered in Claudia's room. We meet there from five-thirty until six on Mondays, Wednesdays, and Fridays, and parents can call us then to set up baby-sitting jobs. That's the BSC in a nutshell, as my mom would say. It's a simple concept, but it works incredibly well. (That day, for example, we'd already taken four calls.) All the members of the club get along really well, so we have a great time — but we're also serious businesswomen (businessgirls?) who know how to make a profitable idea work.

The idea for the BSC, by the way, was Kristy's. That's Kristy Thomas, the president of our club. The one who was trying to convince us to go on a sleigh ride.

"Did you say *sleigh* ride or *hay* ride?" asked Claudia, who is our vice-president. She was sitting cross-legged on her bed, embroidering a sunflower onto a denim shirt.

"Well, it could be either," said Kristy. "It depends on the weather. If there's snow, we'll be on a sleigh with runners, but if not, it'll be a regular hay ride, on a wagon with wheels."

"And are you sure it's free?" I asked. I'm the treasurer of the BSC (did I mention that math is my favorite subject?), and money matters concern me.

"Definitely," said Kristy. "A client of Watson's gave it to him as a holiday gift. Watson said he was *way* too busy to take a sleigh ride — he's been working really hard lately — and Sam and Charlie thought the idea was totally dorky, so Watson offered it to us."

Before I go any further, maybe I'd better explain who Watson, Sam, and Charlie are. Sam and Charlie are Kristy's older brothers (she has a younger one, too, named David Michael), and Watson (whose last name is Brewer) is her stepfather. Not long ago, Kristy's mom got married again after many years of working hard to raise four kids on her own. (Kristy's dad walked out on the family a long time ago. It's not something she talks about much.)

After the wedding, Watson, who happens to be mega-rich, moved the Thomas family across town to live in his mansion. He has two kids from his first marriage: a boy named Andrew and a girl named Karen. They live at the mansion every other month. Big family, right? Well, I'm not done yet. Watson and Kristy's mom decided they wanted to raise a baby together, so they adopted Emily Michelle, who's Vietnamese. She's a toddler, and the family adores her. And once Emily Michelle arrived, Kristy's grandmother Nannie moved in, too, just to help out. Also, in case you think the mansion might still be a little empty, there are a bunch of pets: a cat, a huge puppy dog, two goldfish, and a rat and a hermit crab. (The last two are only there when Andrew and Karen are.)

Kristy's family life may be kind of on the chaotic side, but Kristy herself is one of the most normal, well-balanced people I know. She's energetic, full of ideas, and just a *little* bossy at times. She has her priorities straight, too: she spends absolutely *no* time on clothes or makeup, since those things aren't important to her. Instead, she uses her time to do things she likes, such as coach a little kids' softball team.

"Um, Kristy, *when* did you say this sleigh — or hay — ride would be?" asked Mary Anne. "If you give me the date, I'll check to see if we're all free." She riffled through the pages of the BSC record book, which she, as club secretary, is in charge of. Her small, neat handwriting is on every page. She keeps track of all of our schedules and can tell at a glance which of us is available when a parent calls to set up a job.

Mary Anne and Kristy are best friends. They *look* a little alike: both of them are on the short side with brown hair and eyes. But other than looks, they don't seem to have much in common. Mary Anne couldn't be bossy if her life depended on it. She's extremely shy, very sentimental, and one of the sweetest people you'll ever meet. She's an only child who was brought up by her dad. (Her mom died when Mary Anne was just a baby.)

"I don't think we *have* a definite date yet," said Kristy. "It would have to be sometime in the next few weeks, I guess, before Christmas."

"I wish Dawn could be here for it," said Mary Anne wistfully. "I miss her so much."

We all miss Dawn. That's Dawn Schafer, Mary Anne's stepsister (and *other* best friend) and another member of the BSC. She's in California now, on an extended visit with her dad and her brother, Jeff. Dawn grew up in California, but when her parents divorced, she and Jeff moved to Stoneybrook with their mom. Mrs. Schafer had grown up in Stoneybrook, so in a way she was coming home.

Soon after Dawn moved here, she and Mary Anne became good friends and found out that their parents had dated way back when they were both students at Stoneybrook High. Dawn and Mary Anne schemed to get the old flames back together, and before long, wedding bells were ringing! (Is that the most romantic story you've ever heard, or *what*?)

Meanwhile, Dawn's brother Jeff had moved back to California to live with his dad (he couldn't *stand* Stoneybrook). And then, not long ago, Dawn realized *she* needed to spend some time out there, too. She'll be back in Stoneybrook soon, I'm sure — but not soon enough for Mary Anne, who looked as if she might cry just *thinking* about Dawn.

When Dawn's here, she's the alternate officer of the BSC. That just means she can step in for any *other* officer who can't make it to a meeting. While she's away, that job is being handled by Shannon Kilbourne, who lives in Kristy's new neighborhood. Shannon's normally one of our *associate* members (Logan Bruno, Mary Anne's steady boyfriend, is the other), so until Dawn left, she didn't attend meetings regularly. (Associate members just stand by to help out when we're swamped with work.) It's been great to have Shannon at our meetings more often, since we've been able to get to know her better. She goes to private school, instead of to SMS, where the rest of us go. Shannon is one of those incredibly good students who get all A's and also manages to take part in every single extracurricular activity. She's pretty, with curly blonde hair (*naturally* curly, unlike mine) and blue eyes. She has two younger sisters, Tiffany and Maria, so she's used to baby-sitting.

"It sounds like fun to me," Shannon said now, talking about the sleigh ride. "I've never done anything like that before."

"I wonder what you *wear* on a sleigh ride?" asked Claudia. "I mean, you want to be warm, but you want to *look* good, too. . . ." She gazed over at her closet. As usual, she was already planning her outfit.

As vice-president of the BSC, Claud doesn't have many official duties. She's v.p. because we meet in her room, and we meet in her room because she's the only member with her own phone line. She has to answer any BSC calls that come in when we're *not* meeting, but that's about it. She does take it upon herself to have snacks on hand for every meeting — that day she had passed around chocolate-covered graham crackers (and Frookies for me) — but that's not an *official* duty.

As treasurer of the club, I *do* have official duties. I keep track of the money we each earn, just so we have a record. Each of us keeps her (or his) own earnings, of course. That is, except for what we pay in dues. I collect dues every Monday (I'd done it at the beginning of that day's meeting), and keep careful accounts of how much money we have in the club treasury. We use the money for things like Claudia's phone bill and Kristy's transportation costs (we pay her brother Charlie to drive her to meetings, now that she lives too far away to walk), and for buying markers and things for our Kid-Kits.

What are Kid-Kits? They're another of Kristy's great ideas. Remember how, when you were little, you'd go over to another kid's house and their toys would be just *fascinating*, even if they weren't brand new? Well, that's the idea behind Kid-Kits. They're boxes we've stuffed with hand-me-down toys, books, and games. Plus we add some new things, like markers and stickers. Then we decorate the boxes to look cool. (Claudia is always changing hers. Last month it looked like a pirate ship, and now it looks like a jeweled handbag.) The kids we sit for go wild when they see us arriving with our Kid-Kits.

As I listened to the others talk about the sleigh ride, I was scribbling in the club notebook, writing up a job I'd had that afternoon. I had been sitting for Jamie Newton, who is one of our favorite charges, and I was making some notes about the cold he's had lately. The club notebook is another of Kristy's ideas. We write about our jobs, and then we read what everyone else has written. The extra work is kind of a pain, but it's worth it, because it means we're totally caught up with what's going on with our clients. I think the parents really appreciate having sitters who are so well-informed.

I finished my notes and passed the notebook to Jessi, who had asked for it earlier. Jessi Ramsey is one of our two junior officers; her best friend Mallory Pike is the other. Unlike the rest of us, who are thirteen and in the eighth grade, Jessi and Mal are eleven and in the sixth. They take a lot of afternoon sitting jobs, since their parents have decreed that they are too young to sit at night for anyone except their own siblings.

According to Jessi and Mal, their parents think they are too young for a *lot* of things. Such as contacts for Mal, who hates her glasses. Or miniskirts for Jessi, who wouldn't mind showing off her beautiful legs.

Jessi's a serious ballet student. She's been

studying *forever*, and I wouldn't be surprised to see her dancing at Lincoln Center someday. (That's the main place to see ballet in New York City.) She's African-American, and has a close, loving family: her parents, her younger sister Becca, her baby brother Squirt (actual name: John Philip Ramsey, Jr.), and her aunt Cecelia, who lives with the family.

Mallory, who has reddish, curly hair, has a close family, too, but it's a lot bigger than Jessi's. In fact, it's bigger than *anyone's*. Mal has *seven* brothers and sisters, all younger than she is. After Mal come Adam, Jordan, and Byron, who are identical triplets. Then there's Vanessa, Nicky, Margo, and Claire, the baby of the family. Life at the Pike house is pretty hectic, most of the time. Mal maintains her peace of mind by escaping to her room to read, write, and sketch. Both she and Jessi love to read, and Mal hopes someday to be a children's book author and illustrator.

Jessi wrote a few sentences in the notebook, and passed it to Mal, who was sitting next to her on the floor. Then she straightened out her legs and leaned her body over them in an impossible-looking ballet stretch. "I'd *love* to go on a sleigh ride," she said, her voice muffled because of the way her face was pressed against her knees. "It sounds like fun. Can't you just *hear* the sleigh bells ringing?"

As if to echo Jessi's question, the phone suddenly started to ring. It rang about six more times before our meeting was over, all calls from parents who wanted to set up jobs. The holiday season is a busy time for us, and I could see that this year would be no exception. But I like being busy: that's what being a member of the BSC is all about. I never understand it when other kids at school complain about being bored. When I listen to them, I realize how lucky I am to have the BSC in my life. Being a member of this club means spending lots of time with a bunch of good friends. It means hanging out with little kids, which is something I adore. It means earning my own spending money. And it means I'm *never* bored!

"Have fun with Zucchini!"

"*Robert!*" I said, giggling. "You know his name is Carrot."

"Carrot, Zucchini, what's the difference?" asked Robert. "Why not Rutabaga?"

I giggled some more and gave Robert a little shove. He shoved me back, and our shoving match turned into a brief hug. "Anyway, have fun," he said. It was Tuesday afternoon, and school had just let out. I was about to head to the Johanssens' for my first day of dog-walking and house-sitting. The Johanssens had left that morning.

"You, too," I answered. "Make a lot of baskets for me."

"Sure," he said. Then he loped off toward his basketball game.

I stood watching him. I like to watch Robert run; he's an excellent athlete, and he looks great when he's in motion. Robert is my boyfriend, and I may be biased, but I think he's about the nicest guy at SMS. He's cute, too. He's tall, with dark brown hair and deep, dark eyes and this killer smile that makes your knees weak. Or, at least, it makes *my* knees weak.

When I first met him, Robert was a star player on the SMS basketball team. I got to know him during a time when I thought I might want to be a cheerleader. I even tried out for the squad. As it turned out, I didn't make the cut, for some pretty creepy reasons. That was the last straw for Robert, who had been feeling more and more fed up with the way athletes and cheerleaders are treated at our school. They are looked up to so much, and both teachers and students treat them as if they are something ultra-special. Anyway, Robert decided he'd had enough, and he quit the basketball team, to the dismay of his coach and his teammates.

Robert and I have been going out ever since then. We've gone through some rocky times — this past summer, for example, when I went a little overboard in my efforts to spend time with him — but we're pretty solid these days. We don't spend tons of time together, though, since we're both very busy. I have BSC meetings and baby-sitting jobs almost every day, and Robert plays basketball regularly with a bunch of guys at the town gym. (That's where he was going that afternoon.) They're planning to start a league, and they're also thinking of sponsoring and coaching a league for younger kids. Robert would be great at that. He's so patient, and he's a good teacher.

Anyway, with all our activities, we mainly see each other when we can grab a few minutes during school, plus we usually go on one date a week, on Friday or Saturday night. Sometimes I wish we could be together more, but I have a feeling it's better this way.

Robert disappeared around the corner, and I turned and headed for the Johanssens'. "Rutabaga awaits!" I said, making myself laugh out loud. Fortunately, nobody saw me. I must have looked pretty silly, talking and laughing as I walked along all by myself.

As soon as I turned onto Kimball Street, I could see the Johanssens' house looking tidy, as always. It sits squarely on its corner lot, with a crabapple tree in its front yard and a welcoming dried-flower wreath on the front door. Looking at the house, I decided that nobody would be able to tell, at a glance, that the Johanssens were away. The curtains were only partly drawn, as always, so the house didn't look shut up. Also, the Johanssens had left their car in the driveway. "To help make it look like somebody's home," Dr. Johanssen had explained to me. "Anyway, it's cheaper to take the train to the airport than it would be to pay for parking there the whole time we'll be gone."

I stopped at the head of the flagstone walk and stuck my hand into the mailbox, which is red, with a painting of a white goose on it. Sure enough, there was a pile of mail sitting inside it. I took it out and carried it up to the front porch, but then I had to set it down on the little bench to the right of the door. Why? Because I'd suddenly remembered that I'd need a key to open the door.

I patted my pockets, trying to remember which one the key was in. As I searched, I began to hear barking from inside, and I knew Carrot had heard me. The barking grew louder and louder as Carrot ran toward the door. "It's okay, Carrot," I called. "It's me, Stacey. I just have to find the key." I looked over my shoulder, to make sure nobody had heard me talking to a dog. I was setting a record for silliness that afternoon.

Finally I found the key, in the inside pocket of my jacket. I stuck it into the lock and turned it, but the door didn't open. I could hear Carrot snuffling and whining a little. I tried the key again, and this time it worked. I pushed the door open and Carrot bounded forward to greet me.

He was *really* wound up. I didn't know why. After all, I figured, he should be used to being by himself all day long, with Dr. Johanssen and her husband at work, and Charlotte at school. (Later, Dr. Johanssen explained that seeing all their suitcases had seemed to set Carrot off. "He always knows when something's up," she said. "He probably thought we were leaving forever and he'd never see another human again.")

Anyway, Carrot was jumping around in circles and making this little crying sound. Every so often he'd jump up on me and try to lick my face. "Hi, Carrot," I said, patting him, "Hi, there, boy. Were you a good dog today?"

I've never had a dog, myself, but I've heard dog owners — Kristy, for example — talk to their dogs, and that's the kind of thing they always say. Carrot seemed to respond well to it, so I kept it up. "Good boy, Carrot," I said. He was still leaping around. "Want to go for a walk?" Carrot ran toward the kitchen and reappeared seconds later with a brown leather leash in his mouth. He trotted over to me and dropped the leash at my feet. Then he sat down, wagged his stubby little tail, and looked at me intently.

I should stop here and describe Carrot. He's a medium-sized gray schnauzer. His coarse hair is short all over, except for on his face, where it's long and stiff, kind of like a big bushy beard and mustache with hair gel in it. He has these funny, spiky eyebrows, too. Carrot is a *muscular* dog. That's the only word I can think of to describe his body. He moves as if he has *springs* inside, all tightly wound. He's not a relaxed, lazy-looking dog like Pow, this basset hound I know. But Carrot has a great personality. He always seems happy and excited, and he loves any kind of attention from people.

I clipped the leash onto Carrot's collar and brought him outside, closing the front door behind me and using the key to lock it again. Then the two of us walked across Kimball Street to this empty lot where the Johanssens always take Carrot to "do his business," as Charlotte says.

He "did his business" pretty quickly, and afterward I walked him around the block, passing the house where I lived for awhile when I first moved to Stoneybrook. (My whole family first moved here from New York when my dad was transferred, and then we moved *back* to the city when my dad was transferred again. Then, after the divorce, my mom decided she wanted to return to Stoneybrook, and I came with her — but we moved into a different house.) Now Jessi and her family live in our first house, which is on Fawcett Avenue, around the corner from Kimball. Actually, you can see the back of Jessi's house from the back of the Johanssens'.

I looked at the house as I went by. Jessi wasn't home; I knew she had a sitting job that afternoon. I thought I might see her sister Becca playing in the yard, but the yard was empty. I realized Becca must feel a little lonely without Charlotte around; the two of them are best friends.

Carrot began to pull on the leash as soon as we got past the Ramseys' house, and I had to trot to keep up with him. "I guess you're ready for your dinner, huh, Carrot?" I asked. He wagged his little tail some more and walked even more quickly. We were back at the Johanssens' in no time, and the minute I unlocked the door, Carrot headed straight for the kitchen and stood waiting near his dog dish.

I checked the page of notes Dr. Johanssen had left me, which was posted on the fridge. "Fill dish three-quarters full," I read. "Add protein powder and water, and stir." I followed the directions, with Carrot watching me hungrily every step of the way. Then I put down his bowl and he started to eat as if he'd never *seen* food before. I guess dogs are just always hungry.

I wandered around the kitchen for a minute. It's small but very efficient-looking, with everything stowed away just so. Then, since Carrot still wasn't done, I headed into the living room to wait for him. I planned to hang out with Carrot for a little while, so he wouldn't feel quite so abandoned. Besides, I'd promised Charlotte I would play with him every day.

To reach the Johanssens' living room, you walk out of the kitchen and through the dining room, turn right, go past the front door and center hallway (where the stairs leading to the second floor are), and turn right again into the living room. All the rooms have white walls and pretty wood floors with richly colored Oriental rugs here and there (except for the kitchen, which has a dark-blue tiled floor). None of the rooms is very big, but they're all cozy and set up very comfortably. The living room, for example, has two overstuffed couches and a comfy chair that face both the fireplace and this gorgeous cabinet next to it that holds the TV and stereo. (Charlotte's Uncle Jerry made it. He must be an excellent furniture maker.)

I sat down on one of the couches to wait for Carrot. Then I popped up, opened the doors of the cabinet, and snapped on the radio. (Dr. Johanssen had told me it was fine to do that.) The house had suddenly begun to feel so quiet it was almost creepy, and I thought it would help to hear another human voice. Sure enough, as soon as I tuned in the local station, WSTO, and heard the afternoon DJ (a guy named Wild Bill), I felt better.

Carrot came trotting in as soon as I sat down again, and I clapped my hands and called him over to me. "Where's your toy, Carrot?" I asked, as Charlotte had instructed me to. "Where's Mister Manny-Man?" Mister Manny-Man is what the Johanssens have named Carrot's favorite toy: a soft white fuzzy doll he loves to chew on and carry around. He even sleeps with it, like a kid with a teddy bear.

Carrot ran to find the toy behind the easy chair. Then he brought it over to me, looking so proud of himself that I almost burst out laughing. "Good boy," I said. "Now, can you say your prayers?"

Carrot put his paws onto my lap and laid his head on top of them. Then he looked up at me with the sweetest expression. This time I *did* burst out laughing. I don't know who taught Carrot to do that, but it's the best dog trick I've ever seen.

Then, in the middle of my laughing fit, I heard something on the radio that made my giggles dry right up. ". . . medium build, red hair . . . be on the alert. . . . may be armed and dangerous." Wild Bill was reading an emergency news bulletin about a convict who had escaped from a nearby prison.

I'll tell you right now that it didn't take me long to finish up my games with Carrot and get out of that empty house, making sure, of course, that I locked everything up tightly behind me.

Back at home, I discovered that my mom had gone out for a business dinner. I called my friends to tell them the news I'd heard, and then I spent an uneasy evening alone in *my* empty house — after checking to make sure *it* was locked up tightly, too. I definitely wasn't interested in any uninvited company!

I woke to bright sunshine on Wednesday morning, and immediately felt a little silly about my nervousness the night before. After all, it was ridiculous to think that an escaped prisoner was going to make a beeline for me, Stacey McGill. As I looked out at the sparkling day (the sky was so clear and blue it almost hurt my eyes) I realized that, chances were, the guy had already been caught.

I checked the thermometer outside my window. "All *right*!" I said to myself, when I saw how cold it was. Finally, I was going to be able to wear my new winter coat. It's stunning, the nicest coat I've ever owned. But I haven't had the chance to wear it yet this year; it's a really *warm* coat, and the weather just hasn't been that cold.

I bounded down the stairs for breakfast, and found my mother frowning over the morning paper. "They haven't caught that prisoner yet," she said, after I'd stopped to kiss her good morning.

"No?" I said, opening the fridge to find milk for my Shredded Wheat.

"I was stopped at a police blockade last night, on my way home," my mom said. "They're working hard to capture this guy. He must be dangerous."

I shrugged. Somehow I just wasn't that worried about him anymore. "They'll catch him soon, I'm sure," I said. I sat down with my bowl of cereal and picked up the second section of the paper so I could check on my horoscope (and Robert's) while I ate.

After breakfast, I realized that I'd better hurry if I wanted to finish my chores at the Johanssens' and still make it to school on time. I ran to the closet and grabbed my new coat. Then I couldn't resist modeling it for my mom. (She'd seen it before — in fact, we bought it at Bellair's with her employee discount.) "First day for the new coat!" I said.

"It really is a lovely one," said my mom, reaching out to touch the furry trim. "You look gorgeous in it, too."

"Thanks," I said. I grabbed my shoulder bag. "See you tonight!"

I ran out the door and started to jog toward the Johanssens', but after about half a block I was already way overheated. That coat was *warm!* I slowed down to a fast walk, and arrived a few minutes later.

The Johanssens' newspaper was sitting on their front doormat. "We *could* stop delivery," Dr. Johanssen had said, "but we'd rather not broadcast it around that we're going to be away for so long." That had made sense to me, and I'd promised to bring it inside first thing every morning.

I stood on the front porch, rummaging through my pockets again for that key. I expected to hear Carrot start barking any minute, the way he had the day before, but there was no noise from inside.

Suddenly, I felt a little nervous.

Maybe I'd relaxed too soon about that escaped prisoner. What if — what if he had ended up at the *Johanssens'* the night before, and discovered that their empty house made a perfect hiding place? What if he was in there right now, waiting for me to walk in? What if he had done something horrible to Carrot?

Finally, I found the key. My hand shook as I put it into the keyhole and turned it. Then I pushed open the door. "Carrot?" I called. My voice came out all quavery.

There was no response.

"Carrot?" I called again, a little more loudly. I stepped to the left and peeked into the living room. No Carrot. I walked to my right and checked the dining room. Carrot was nowhere in sight.

I felt a shiver go down my spine, and pulled my coat closer around me.

"Carrot?" I called one more time. This time I was practically yelling.

From upstairs, I heard the sound of floorboards creaking. My heart started to pound, but before I became *really* frightened, I looked up the stairs and saw Carrot poking his nose around the bannister. He looked very sleepy.

In fact, he looked so much like a person who had just woken up that I had to giggle. "Sorry, Carrot," I said. "Didn't mean to *wake* you." I'd totally forgotten what Dr. Johanssen had told me about Carrot always sleeping later than everybody else in the family.

Carrot came down the stairs a little stiffly. "Boy, am I glad to see *you*," I told him, as he yawned and stretched. He sniffed my hand and wagged his tail.

"Looks like you were a good boy," I said. "Were you good?" I walked with him through the downstairs, checking each room. There were no signs of misbehavior. No signs, that is, until I went into the kitchen for his leash and found a chewed-up piece of paper littering one corner of the floor. Carrot must have pulled an old envelope or something out of the wastebasket and had a little fun with it.

"Oh, Carrot," I said in a scolding voice. I pointed to the paper. "Did you do that?"

Carrot put his head down and looked so ashamed that I felt sorry for him.

I picked up the paper and threw it away. Then I turned to Carrot. "It's no big deal," I said, patting him. "It's okay."

As soon as Carrot heard the word "okay," he licked my hand and started to look happier. Then, when I picked up his leash, he looked *really* happy. In fact, he danced around so much I had trouble clipping the leash onto his collar.

Since I had to move fast if I wanted to be on time for homeroom, I took Carrot for a quick walk, fed him, gave him one last pat as he gobbled down his food, and left. I figured I'd spend some time playing with him that afternoon, when I returned after school.

As it turned out, Carrot had other ideas.

When I let myself back into the Johanssens' house later that day, I discovered that Carrot had decided not to wait for *me* to play. It was obvious right away, the second I stepped inside, that Carrot had played by himself all day long. And from the looks of things, he'd had a pretty good time.

"Oh, Carrot," I said, dismayed. The house was a mess. Bits and scraps of paper lay all over the floor. A small running shoe that must have been Charlotte's sat in a soggy, chewed-up lump near the bottom of the stairs. And when I looked into the dining room, I saw chew marks all down one of the legs of the beautiful big table that takes up most of the room.

I heard doggy footsteps on the second floor, and looked up the stairs to see Carrot standing on the landing, giving me this pleading, guilty look and wagging his tail ever so slightly. "Bad dog, Carrot," I said firmly. Carrot slunk away from the landing. I walked up the steps and found him under Mr. Johanssen's desk, which sits at the top of the stairs. Carrot has a bed under that desk, because, as Dr. Johanssen told me, "he likes little cave-like spaces."

I bent to look under the desk and saw that Carrot had brought even *more* chewed-up stuff onto his bed. It looked as if he'd torn into a whole box of tissues. "Carrot!" I said. He gave me that pleading look again.

"Oh, all right," I said, crouching to pick up some of the scraps of tissue. "I know it's only because you're upset about them leaving. It's okay." It *wasn't* exactly okay — I mean, it made me kind of nervous that he was carrying on that way — but I knew I had to reassure Carrot or he'd probably only do it again.

Once again, as soon as he heard the word

"okay," Carrot perked right up. He crawled out from under the desk and gave me a big, sloppy kiss. His mustache tickled so much I had to giggle.

"Okay, okay," I said, sitting back on the floor with a thump as Carrot nuzzled me. Every time I said "okay," he kissed me again. Soon I was laughing so hard I forgot to be mad, which was probably Carrot's goal. Finally, I caught my breath and stood up. "Ready to go out?" I asked him.

Believe me, I have *never* had so many conversations with somebody who couldn't talk back! But I was getting used to talking to Carrot, and he *did* always respond, in his own doggy way.

I spent a couple of hours at the Johanssens' that afternoon, playing with Carrot and cleaning up the mess he'd made. And when it was time to go, I had a long talk with him about how he'd better be good or else he wouldn't be getting any Milkbones. From the way he looked at me, I was pretty sure we had an understanding.

". . . plus one of Charlotte's *shoes*, and a whole box of tissues!" It was late that afternoon, and I was in Claud's room for our Wednesday BSC meeting. I was telling my friends about Carrot's escapades that day, and

I had them all laughing. Like me, they'd been a little nervous about the escaped prisoner, so it felt good to laugh. By that time, of course, the whole thing *did* seem pretty funny.

Kristy had a few pointers for me on how to deal with a misbehaving dog (she's used to this chewing thing, since she lives with a puppy), and Jessi suggested that I bring Carrot some special treats, "so he knows somebody still loves him." I thanked them both, but I was pretty sure that Carrot wasn't going to be that bad again. As I said, we had an understanding.

A little later on in the meeting, Kristy came up with yet another of her fabulous ideas. It was right after we'd arranged a whole series of jobs with some of our favorite clients. We had started to talk about how it would be nice to do something special for the kids around the holidays.

"But Hanukkah is already over — it was so early this year — and Christmas is only a few weeks away," said Jessi. "How can we plan something with so little time?"

"I've got it!" said Kristy. "The sleigh ride! I mean, the *hay* ride! Oh, whatever. I mean, why don't we take the *kids* on that ride? They'd love it!"

"Great idea," said Mary Anne, right away. "And maybe afterward we could have a little party for them, in the barn at my house. You know, with refreshments and games and things."

"I love it!" said Claudia. "Let's make it a definite plan."

That was it! The whole thing was decided in about ten seconds. I knew the kids would love the idea, including Charlotte; the date we picked meant she would be back in time to attend. Our party would be the perfect holiday treat for all our favorite kids.

Thursday

Me and my big mouth! Why can't I think before I start talking? I know, I know, you guys are always telling me this. So is my mom. And I try, I really do try. Believe it or not, there are times when I stop myself just in time, before I say something dumb. But this time wasn't one of them. It all started because I was excited about our plans for the kids' holiday party...

Kristy was really disgusted with herself. If there's one thing she hates, it's breaking a promise she's made to a kid. And thanks to her big mouth, she was facing the possibility of breaking a promise to a whole *bunch* of kids!

Here's how it happened:

Kristy had a Thursday afternoon sitting job with the Arnold twins, Carolyn and Marilyn, who're eight. They're identical: both of them have brown hair and sparkling brown eyes. They used to dress alike, but lately they've developed separate styles which reflect their individuality. It used to be nearly impossible to tell them apart — unless you spotted the tiny mole under Marilyn's right eye — but now it's no problem at all.

Marilyn, who is a serious piano student, still has the "bowl" haircut that both twins used to have, only now it's grown out a few inches. She wears simple, comfortable clothes most of the time.

Carolyn, on the other hand, is more like a junior version of Claud and me. She has a very stylish haircut (short in front, with longer curls down the back), and she loves trendy clothes and accessories. But she's no airhead: she also loves science and is always involved in some project or other.

That afternoon, when she arrived at the Arnolds' door, Kristy had a feeling there were *lots* of projects going on in that house, but that they weren't exactly *scientific* ones.

Her first clue was the wreath on the door. Obviously handmade with loving care, it was a thing of beauty. Someone had used five different kinds of greens, interwoven them with red berries and gold pine cones, and topped the wreath off with a red velvet ribbon. As soon as Kristy saw it, she remembered what Christmas is like in the Arnold household.

Mrs. Arnold is one of those people who throws herself into the holiday season, and Marilyn and Carolyn love it, too. Their house is always fully decorated with lights (Mr. Arnold's contribution), starting on the day after Thanksgiving. Then, during the time leading up to Christmas, the family continues to decorate the house to within an inch of its life.

There are snowflake stencils on the windows, and red and green candles on the mantelpiece, and always a gorgeous tree (*dripping* with handmade and store-bought ornaments) in the family room. Every side table in the house is covered with Christmas crafts, such as a nativity scene made from spools and fabric remnants, or a Frosty the Snowman made out of Styrofoam balls.

The house always *smells* like Christmas, too, since Mrs. Arnold makes it a point to turn out at least two batches of cookies a day. She gives them away to friends and to the mailman and the girl who delivers the paper.

In fact, when she greeted Kristy at the door that day, she was holding a large round tin box decorated with a winter skating scene. "I wanted to be sure to give you these now," she said, handing the box to Kristy, "so I don't forget. They're for you and your friends — just as a thank you for all the wonderful sitting you do."

"Wow!" said Kristy, taking the tin and opening it up to look inside. "Thanks! There must be ten different kinds of cookies in here."

"Well, I always like to try some new recipes," said Mrs. Arnold. "But I love to make the traditional ones, too."

"Like chocolate chip!" said Marilyn, appearing behind her mother.

"And don't forget peanut butter," added Carolyn. "Santa's favorite."

Marilyn grinned up at Kristy. "We know Santa's just for *little* kids," she said. "But we still like to leave cookies and milk out for him and the reindeer — just in case."

"And the cookies *always* get eaten," Carolyn added.

"Hmmm," said Kristy, raising an eyebrow. "Very mysterious!"

Both girls giggled, and Mrs. Arnold smiled.

"Well, I'm off," she said , putting on her coat. "Why don't you girls show Kristy our tree?"

The twins were so enthusiastic about the idea that they barely said good-bye to their mom. They each grabbed one of Kristy's hands and dragged her down the hall.

"Close your eyes!" demanded Marilyn.

"We'll tell you when to open them," said Carolyn.

Kristy stood with her eyes shut tight and listened to a whispered conference as the twins decided which of them should plug in the lights and which of them should lead Kristy into the room. After a few seconds, Kristy felt someone tugging on her sleeve and pulling her into the family room.

"Okay!" cried both twins at once.

"Open your eyes," added Carolyn.

Kristy opened her eyes. "Wow!" she said. She had been prepared to gush over the tree, since she knew how important it was to the girls, but as soon as she saw it she realized she wouldn't have to *pretend* to be enthusiastic. The tree looked spectacular, like something out of a story book. It was tall and full, with long, bluish-green needles. And it was covered with hundreds of tiny, sparkling white lights, ropes of cranberries and popcorn, and beautiful ornaments — some that the family had made and some they'd collected over the years.

"It's the best tree we've ever had," said Carolyn.

"The biggest and the best," echoed Marilyn.

"It's really beautiful," said Kristy. "You guys did a great job."

"Mom and Dad did a lot of it, but we helped to string the popcorn and cranberries," said Marilyn.

"Plus, we made some of the ornaments," Marilyn added. "See this one?" She pointed to a satiny red ball with a motif of dancing musical notes running around the middle. "I made that in art class."

"And I made this one," said Carolyn, pointing to a neon-colored ornament that looked like something a rock star would wear as an earring.

"I love them both," said Kristy. "You guys sure do like the holidays, don't you?"

"Definitely," said Marilyn.

"They're the best," said Carolyn.

"Then maybe you'd like to hear about the special holiday party my friends and I are planning for you and the other kids we sit for," Kristy said teasingly. As soon as she said it, she told me later, she realized maybe she shouldn't have. After all, plans for the party weren't exactly finalized yet. But once the words were out of her mouth, it was too late to take them back.

"Party?" asked Carolyn, her eyes lighting up. "When?"

"What *kind* of party?" asked Marilyn eagerly.

"Well, it'll be sometime in the next couple of weeks. Part of it will be outdoors," said Kristy, "and part of it will be in Mary Anne's barn. We'll have food and games and things in the barn."

"What about the outdoor part?" asked Carolyn.

"Well," said Kristy, "that's sort of a surprise." She was hoping the girls might let the subject drop.

"Oh, please tell us," said Marilyn. *"Please."*

Kristy tried to keep from spilling the beans, but the twins were incredibly persistent. Finally, she broke down and told them about the sleigh ride. "Or it might be a *hay* ride," Kristy added, "depending on the weather."

But the twins didn't seem to hear that part. As soon as they heard the words "sleigh ride," they went nuts. "I *always* wanted to do that," said Carolyn. "Just think, we'll be riding along, skimming over the snow."

"The bells on the horses will be jingling,"

said Marilyn dreamily, "and we'll be all wrapped up in cozy blankets, just like in a Laura Ingalls Wilder book."

"Well, we *might* not — " Kristy began, but the girls ignored her. They were too busy talking about how wonderful the sleigh ride would be. Kristy shook her head in dismay. The twins hadn't paid attention to the fact that there would only be a *sleigh* ride if it snowed in time. And you can never be sure if there will be a white Christmas in Stoneybrook.

Kristy shrugged. She could already see there was no way to clue the twins in to the reality of the situation; they were too far gone with their Winter Wonderland fantasies. "Hey, how about some hot chocolate?" she asked, hoping to distract them.

"Great!" said Marilyn.

"With marshmallows?" asked Carolyn.

"Sure," said Kristy. She headed for the kitchen to whip up the cocoa, leaving the twins in the family room discussing the sleigh ride. Kristy knew she should have kept her mouth shut about the party, but as she stirred up the hot chocolate she convinced herself that it wasn't as if she'd told *everybody*. It was only the twins who knew, and only the twins who would end up disappointed if there were no snow.

"Here we go!" she said cheerfully, as she

came back into the family room with two steaming mugs.

"Yum!" said Carolyn, taking one of the mugs.

"Where's Marilyn?" asked Kristy.

"She went to find the Kuhns' number," said Carolyn. "They're the only ones we haven't called yet. We've told everybody else."

"What?" asked Kristy. She had a sinking feeling in her stomach. ("Just like when you're in an elevator and it zooms up about ten floors," she told me later.)

Marilyn came back into the room waving a piece of paper. "Here it is!" she said. "Oh, thanks for the cocoa," she added, picking up her cup.

"Um," Kristy began. "When you said you told everyone, what exactly did you mean?"

"We told them about the sleigh ride!" Marilyn said. She was dialing the phone as she spoke.

"Told *who*?" asked Kristy. The sinking sensation hadn't stopped. It was as if the elevator were on the hundredth floor and still climbing.

"The Braddocks, the Barretts, the Pikes . . ." said Carolyn, counting on her fingers.

"Don't forget the Rodowskys!" Marilyn said. Then she hung up the phone. "Nobody's home at the Kuhns', I guess."

"Ohh, no," said Kristy, under her breath,

as the realization of what had happened sunk in. Practically every one of the BSC's regular charges was now looking forward to a holiday sleigh ride, and every one of those kids might very well end up disappointed.

But there was nothing she could do about it. All she could do was distract Marilyn and Carolyn, so that they wouldn't do any further damage. "How about if you guys help me make the invitations?" she asked. Soon all three of them were working busily at the kitchen table, which was covered with glitter, scraps of construction paper, and crayons. They ended up with a pile of invitations, Kristy said, but she wasn't sure how distracted the twins were. For one thing, they talked excitedly about the sleigh ride the whole time. And for another thing, every single invitation the twins made featured a carefully colored picture of a bunch of kids riding happily over the snow on a sleigh.

While Kristy was over at the Arnolds', dealing with the results of her big mouth, I was at the Johanssens', busy with Carrot. My job there was going well for the most part, but I was beginning to learn a few things about house-and-pet-sitting.

For starters, it's a big responsibility. People are counting on you to take good care of things that are really important to them: in my case, a house and a dog. You can't shrug off the job when you don't feel like doing it, or put it aside until a more convenient moment. It's like baby-sitting that way, I guess.

I mean, Carrot could *survive* for an extra few hours if I didn't show up right after school. He could use his dog door to go outside and "take care of business," and he probably wouldn't notice if his afternoon meal was a little late.

On the other hand, the Johanssens were

counting on me — and *paying* me — to give Carrot the attention he needs. Dr. Johanssen had explained to me that for most dogs, and definitely for Carrot, the most important thing in life is to be with people. Preferably the people you *belong* to, but in a pinch any old person will do.

(The second-most important thing is food. Dogs are *always* hungry.)

So I was very aware, all through my days at school, that Carrot was sitting at home in an empty house, watching and waiting for a human to come and pat him and play with him. That was why it wasn't *too* hard to resist when Robert asked me to go out for a slice of pizza after school, or when Claud suggested we do some Christmas shopping together at the mall. I'd be tempted for just a second, and then I'd think of Carrot's furry face wearing that quizzical "don't you love me?" expression, and it would be easy to say no to my friends.

Another thing I was learning about house-and-pet-sitting was that, while it was a fun thing to do for a *little* while, I wouldn't want to do it all the time. It's just not as much *fun* as being with kids. Yes, it was true that I could play tug-of-war with Carrot for what seemed like hours, without feeling too bored. But face it, dogs can't talk. They can't say funny things or tell you they love you or ask you for a hug, the way kids can. So, as much as I liked Carrot, I really missed sitting for *humans* — especially for Charlotte. (I was missing her a lot, since I was in her house every day.)

And the last thing about house-and-pet-sitting? Well, it was this: I had thought that taking care of someone's home would be interesting and fun. It might be like playing house; I expected to spend a certain amount of time hanging out there and fantasizing about it being *my* house. But it wasn't really like that. Instead, what it *was*, was a little scary.

Now, I'm not like Mary Anne, who gets spooked if you say "boo" to her in broad daylight. I can deal with watching scary movies or listening to ghost stories. I'm generally pretty brave about things like that. But you know what? Being in that empty house, all by myself, was really starting to make me feel jumpy. I had been just a tiny bit nervous whenever I was there, right from the start. But toward the end of the week, and on into the weekend, I began to feel more and more uneasy.

And it wasn't all in my mind.

There were troubling things happening in that house; things that made me feel *more* than just a tiny bit nervous. But they didn't start happening right away. In fact, right up until Thursday afternoon, everything was totally fine.

I'd stopped by the Johanssens' on Thursday morning before school. Carrot was delighted to see me, and as far as I could tell he'd been good during the night. Oh, there were one or two shredded Kleenexes on the bathroom floor upstairs, but other than that he hadn't gotten into any trouble. I told him he was a good boy, took him for a walk, gave him breakfast, and promised I'd be back as soon as I could.

By the way, the look he gave me as I left that morning could have melted a heart of stone. As soon as he saw me heading for the door, he put on this expression that told me, as clearly as if he'd said it, that he couldn't *believe* I was going to leave him alone all day. His pleading eyes made me feel like the crummiest person in the world as I shut the door and tiptoed away. Fortunately, Dr. Johanssen had warned me about his "act," and she'd assured me that as soon as I left he'd head for his bed, where he'd curl up and sleep for most of the day.

Well, he probably spent *some* time sleeping that Thursday, but he was definitely awake and alert when I came back.

Awake, alert, and *growling*.

That's right, growling. Carrot, the sweet-tempered dog I'd begun to think of as a pal, stood there at the door with the fur on his back all raised up, and *growled* at me when I let myself in that afternoon.

"What's the *matter*?" I asked him. I had shut the front door behind me, and now I kind of flattened myself against it. The growling sound was scary; I didn't know what to expect. Carrot looked as if he meant business. "Carrot?" I said, surprised at how trembly my voice suddenly sounded.

The second he heard his name, he seemed to relax. He looked at my face and I swear his eyes lit up when he recognized me. He sniffed my hand, probably to make sure it really belonged to me, and then gave it a little lick as if he were apologizing for growling at me.

"It's okay, boy," I said, giving him a pat.

He started to wag his tail — *hard* — and soon it was as if his whole body were wagging. He panted and grinned (really!) and jumped around in circles. "That's the Carrot *I* know," I said. "Ready for a walk?"

He ran to the kitchen to fetch his leash, and I followed behind, checking for signs that he'd been chewing on things that day. I saw nothing out of order as we passed through the dining room, and the kitchen looked fine, too, when I gave it a quick glance.

I clipped on Carrot's leash and we headed

outside. It was a nice day for December. The sky was blue and the air was brisk, but not too cold. Not cold enough to make me wish I'd worn my new coat, anyway.

I let Carrot lead me wherever he wanted to go, and we ended up taking a fairly long walk all around the neighborhood. We ran into several people who seemed to know him, including the mail carrier. Carrot recognized her from half a block away, and pulled so hard on the leash that I thought I was going to end up being dragged along the street. When we met on the sidewalk, I found out why.

"Hey, Carrot," the mail carrier said. "How's my boy today?" As she spoke, she was digging into her bag. Carrot stared intently at the bag, wagging his tail. When the woman pulled her hand out, there was a dog biscuit in it. Carrot sat down promptly and put out his paw.

"I don't even have to tell him to sit and shake anymore," said the mail carrier, laughing. She tossed the biscuit to Carrot, who wolfed it down and looked up expectantly.

"That's all for today," she said. "See you tomorrow, Carrot!" She smiled at me. "Dr. Johanssen told me I'd be seeing somebody new walking Carrot," she said. "Have fun with him. He's a good dog. And believe me, I see a *lot* of dogs. I know a good one when I see it." Then she hitched up her mailbag, gave

Carrot a pat and me a wave, and headed on down the street.

Carrot looked disappointed about not getting another biscuit, I thought. But soon he noticed a squirrel on a nearby lawn and seemed to forget about the mail carrier.

Back at the Johanssens', I fixed Carrot's dinner, scooping the food out of a big bin inside the basement door and adding the protein powder, which the Johanssens keep in the fridge. Soon Carrot was standing over his food, eating it in gulps. I went over to the sink to wash the spoon I'd used to scoop out the powder, and that's when I noticed something strange.

There was a glass in the sink, a tall juice glass. It had a small amount of water in the bottom: melted ice cubes, maybe.

I know, I know. What's so weird about a glass? Well, nothing. Unless it's a glass that you didn't use and that wasn't there the day before — and you're the only person who's been in the house.

I stared at it, bewildered. Maybe I was wrong. Maybe it had been there all along. Or else maybe I *had* used it, and forgotten.

Anyway, it wasn't that big a deal. I gave the glass one more glance and shrugged. Then I went through my nighttime routine with Carrot. I made sure his water dish was full, showed him where Mister Manny-Man was hiding (under the dining room table), and gave him a scratch behind the ears. "See you tomorrow," I said. He gave me that sad look again, but I knew he'd be fine.

He was, too. But over the next few days, weird things kept happening every time I went to the Johanssens'.

On Friday morning, I noticed that the coffeemaker was warm. (I had shoved it aside to make room on the counter for Carrot's water dish, which I had just rinsed out.) I didn't wonder too much about that, though. I figured maybe it was on a timer, like the lights that were rigged up to go off and on.

Then, on Friday afternoon, I saw some crumpled Kleenexes in the wastebasket near the TV cabinet in the living room. I could have *sworn* I'd emptied all the wastebaskets after Carrot chewed up those Kleenexes the day before. And when I went to find Carrot's leash, it was missing. Finally I found it — or, rather, *he* did — on the hook by the back door. I was *sure* I'd put it on its regular hook, but I guess I hadn't.

I know these things don't sound too creepy by themselves, but all together they were beginning to give me the willies. Something strange was going on in that house, and I wasn't so sure I wanted to know what it was!

On Saturday morning, the house seemed normal — except for a slight smell of toast lingering in the kitchen. I took Carrot for a *really* long walk, since I knew I'd be rushing when I came back later that day. (I had a date with Robert that evening, and I wanted plenty of time to figure out what to wear.)

Carrot always seemed happy to see me, and he never growled at me again. And I liked him a lot, too. Maybe house-and-pet-sitting was an okay job after all. True, the weird things that had been happening were making me nervous, but then again, I was fairly certain that nobody had broken into the house or anything. I decided to try to relax and enjoy the job for the next week.

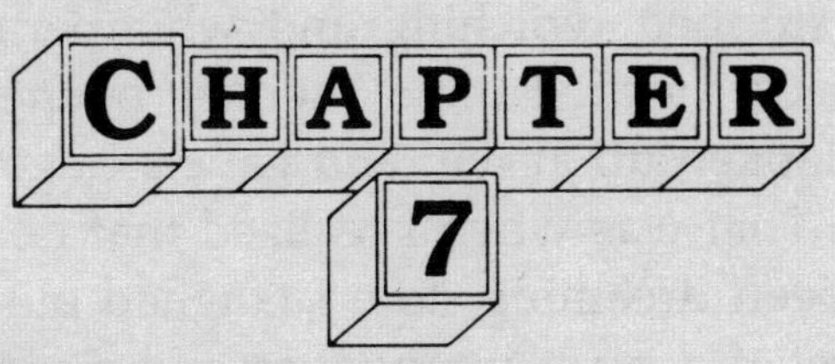

My resolution to relax and enjoy lasted for exactly one day: Sunday. For that one day, everything seemed normal at the Johanssens'. I got there a little late on Sunday morning, but Carrot was waiting patiently. There were no empty glasses in the sink and no Kleenexes in the wastebaskets. The Sunday paper had arrived, and after I'd walked and fed and played with Carrot, I sat down in the living room to read the comics. I was *so* relaxed at the Johanssens' that morning that I actually dozed off in the big easy chair. Carrot, who was lying on the rug nearby, dozed off too.

I woke up first and sat quietly for a moment, savoring the dream I'd just had about Robert and me on the beach at sunset. I *love* dreamy dreams like that.

Then I heard a whimpering sound, and I looked down at Carrot. His eyes were shut tight, but his legs were twitching and he was whining. "Oh, my lord!" I said, putting my hand over my mouth. It looked as if Carrot were having some kind of fit. I reached out to touch him. "Carrot?" I said. "Are you okay?"

He stopped twitching and whimpering as soon as I touched him. Then he opened his eyes, looked up at me, and gave a huge pink yawn. That was when I realized that he must have been dreaming, too. I laughed out loud with relief. Carrot jumped up and ran to get Mister Manny-Man, and we spent the next half hour playing tug-of-war.

(Later that day, when I called to ask her about it, Kristy assured me that Carrot probably *had* been dreaming. "Louie used to do that," she said, talking about her last dog, a collie who died not too long ago. "I always thought he was dreaming about chasing rabbits.")

Anyway, things were fine at the Johanssens' that Sunday morning, and nothing weird happened when I went back that evening, either. Monday morning was fine, too. I had almost forgotten about being creeped out the week before.

But then, on Monday afternoon, something happened that made all those feelings come back. And what followed on Tuesday morning only made me feel more uneasy.

Here's how it began: On Monday, after

school, I headed straight to the Johanssens'. I had already stopped at the mailbox to pull out the mail, and I was standing on the front porch, doing my usual "find-the-key" routine, when I heard a rustling in the bushes to my left. I guess I wasn't all *that* relaxed, because as soon as I heard the noise, I got this shivery feeling all over and I felt the little hairs on the back of my neck stand straight up.

I peered through the latticework of the front porch, telling myself to calm down. "It's probably just a squirrel or something," I muttered to myself.

"Wrong!" called out a cheerful voice. "I'm small, but not *that* small."

My eyes widened as I watched a petite, slim woman with a mass of curly red hair climb out of the bushes near the corner of the house. "Don't worry," she said, with a smile. She must have noticed the horror-stricken look on my face. "I was just reading your meter." She held up a clipboard.

"Ohh," I said, letting out a huge breath. "The meter. Right."

"I *love* your house," said the woman. "It's definitely the cutest one on my route. Have you lived here long?"

"Um, no," I said. My heart was finally beginning to beat at a normal speed. "Actually, I don't live here at all. I'm just house-sitting."

The second the words were out of my mouth, I knew I'd said the wrong thing. I could have kicked myself.

The whole point of having a house-sitter is to make it look as if somebody's home when, in fact, nobody is. And here I was, blabbing to a total stranger, telling her that the Johanssens were away. For all I knew, she was some criminal who was casing the joint for a big robbery.

"I mean," I said, trying frantically to think of some way to take back what I'd just told her, "the owners are *around* — they might be back any minute, even — but I'm kind of watching the house, just to be on the safe side." I stopped short and blushed. I could tell by the way she was looking at me that I had been babbling. What I had just said probably made no sense whatsoever.

"Anyway," I said, trying to act normal, "is everything okay?" I gestured toward the meter.

"Oh, sure," she said. She tucked her clipboard under her arm and turned to go. Just then, I heard a horn honking from around the corner. The woman frowned and tossed back her hair. "That's Joe," she explained, looking back at me and rolling her eyes. "My work partner — and also my husband. He gets a little impatient sometimes." She heaved a sigh. "Take my advice and never get mixed up romantically with somebody you work with."

"I won't," I promised, just to say *something*. Then the honking started up again, and the red-haired woman gave me a little wave and trotted around the corner.

I watched her go. Then I shrugged, stuck the key in the lock, and opened the Johanssens' front door. Carrot was waiting just inside, sitting alertly with his ears up, as if he'd been listening to my conversation with the meter reader. "Hi, Carrot," I said, giving him a pat on the head. He wagged his little tail and poked his wet snuffly nose into my hand.

I gave a quick glance around the downstairs — what I could see of it from the entryway — and saw that everything seemed to be in order. "Ready to go outside?" I asked Carrot.

As always, that question made him very happy and *very* excited. He ran off to find his leash and returned within seconds, dragging it along behind him. I clipped it to his collar and followed him out the door.

Instead of pulling me straight across the street as he usually did, Carrot headed around the corner. It was almost as if he wanted to check something out.

As soon as we turned the corner, I found out what Carrot was after. There was a white van, facing toward me, parked on the side of the street. A green-and-blue symbol was painted on its front and side, and two people were sitting in it: a man with dark hair and a mustache, and a woman with — you guessed it — a head full of red curls. My meter reader. The two of them were just sitting there in the van, talking. Well, to be honest, they were fighting. From where I was standing, I couldn't make out exactly what they were saying, but I could tell by the tone of their voices that they weren't exchanging compliments.

"Come on, Carrot," I said, tugging him back toward our usual walking spot. I didn't like standing there staring at the people in the van, even though I was pretty sure they were too busy arguing to have noticed me.

But Carrot wasn't listening to me. He was interested in that van, and nothing I said or did was going to keep him away from it. When I spoke, he just laid his ears back as if to say, "I can't *hear* you," and when I tugged on the leash he planted his feet and tugged back even harder. I'd never realized before just how strong a dog can be, especially one as stubborn as Carrot.

"Okay, okay," I said grudgingly. I let him lead me down the sidewalk. As we approached the van, I tried not to look at the people in it. I didn't want them to think I was poking my nose into their business. I also tried to put this look on my face that said "walking this way wasn't *my* idea." Carrot, meanwhile, pranced closer and closer to the van.

Finally, we walked by the side door and I sighed with relief, happy to have passed by. I'd been able to hear a few words of the argument, and I didn't really want to hear more. It's *embarrassing* to overhear people fighting about personal stuff.

Unfortunately, Carrot chose the next moment to do something that was beyond embarrassing. In fact, it was humiliating.

He started out by sniffing the rear tire of the van. I could still hear the people arguing, so I gave Carrot a little tug, trying to move him along. But Carrot stood firm, sniffing and sniffing. I'll bet you can guess what he did next.

Right. He lifted his leg.

I wanted to die. I wanted to melt right into the sidewalk. I wanted to become totally invisible. But since I couldn't do any of those things, I did the only thing I *could* do. I turned my eyes to the sky, folded my arms, and waited, hoping that the people in the van wouldn't look out their window and see what was going on.

Luckily for me, they seemed to be completely involved in their fight. In fact, just as Carrot was finishing up, *they* finished up, too.

Here's how the end of the argument went (I could hear every single word): The red-haired woman said, "That's it, Joe. I've really had it this time. I'm moving out." Joe said, in a really nasty, sarcastic voice, "Right. Where to?" And she answered, "Oh, I'll find a place." She sounded calm all of a sudden, and very definite about her plans.

And that was it. Joe started up the van and took off with a squeal of tires. Carrot jumped back onto the sidewalk and stood there trembling. I patted him gently while I watched the van drive off. I shook my head, thinking how strange the episode had been. Who *were* those people? Had the red-haired woman really been reading meters — or was she just checking out the house? For some reason, the incident left me feeling shaken.

That partly explains why what happened on Tuesday morning made me more uneasy, even though it may not sound like much. Here's what happened: When I arrived at the Johannsens' that morning, I couldn't find the newspaper. I glanced over at the neighbors' house and saw *their* paper lying on the steps, so I figured the delivery person had already come by. But the Johanssens' paper was nowhere in sight.

As I walked Carrot, I thought it over, and by the time we went back inside I'd decided what to do. While Carrot was eating the breakfast I'd given him, I grabbed the phone and called the offices of the *Stoneybrook News*. I knew the Johanssens hadn't canceled their paper because they didn't want to announce that they'd be away, so I pretended to be a member of the family. After putting me on hold while he did some checking, the person on the other end assured me that the paper had been delivered as usual.

I hung up and looked down at Carrot. "Something weird is going on," I told him. He cocked his head and gave me a questioning look. "I don't know what it is," I said, "but it's beginning to seem as if something strange happens every single time I come to this house. I'm starting to think I have a mystery on my hands."

Carrot put his nose into my hand, as if to reassure me, but it was going to take more than that to make me feel better. It was time for me to turn to my friends in the BSC.

By the time I went to bed on Tuesday night, I had made a decision. I was going to approach the mystery at the Johanssens' (if it *was* a mystery) in an organized, scientific way. Creepy things had been happening, but I didn't want the situation to get the better of me. So, instead of panicking, I made a plan.

First of all, I wrote down every weird thing that I could remember happening at the house. When I looked at the final list, I was amazed; there were *nine* items on it! In a strange way, putting that list together made me feel better. I'd been a little worried that I might be overreacting, but *anyone* would have to agree that nine weird things in a week is a lot.

The next thing I did was this: I decided to keep the mystery to myself until I could explain it to all my friends at one time. I didn't want to have to go over that list more than once. Also, I wanted to make sure everyone was really paying attention to what I was telling them. My friends in the BSC are *great* at solving mysteries, when they concentrate. Anyway, instead of trying to talk to my friends during lunchtime at school (where I'd probably be interrupted by a cafeteria-wide food fight or by Kristy's gross comments on what the meatloaf resembled), I'd decided to ask Kristy if I could be on the agenda at our BSC meeting that Wednesday afternoon.

I slept well Tuesday night. Coming up with a plan had made me feel much calmer. And on Wednesday morning, when I went to the Johanssens', everything seemed fine.

Well, almost everything.

There was just one thing that bothered me: that glass was in the sink again. I could have *sworn* I had washed it out and left it in the dish drainer to dry. I stared at it for a couple of seconds, while Carrot danced around begging to go out. Then I told myself that maybe I'd only *meant* to wash the glass, but had never actually gotten around to *doing* it.

After a quick walk, I gave Carrot breakfast and said good-bye. As usual, he seemed very sorry to see me go. I was getting used to that pitiful, pleading look he always gave me as I left the house, but it was still hard to close the door on him.

Even though nothing too strange had happened in the house that morning, I still felt uneasy. I spent the whole day at school walking around in a fog. None of my friends seemed to notice much, though. When I saw them at lunchtime they were too busy watching Alan Gray (the most obnoxious boy in our school) as he sculpted a snowman with his mashed potatoes.

("Didn't anybody ever tell him you're not supposed to play with your food?" Mary Anne had asked, wrinkling her nose. "What *else* can we do with it?" Kristy had answered, staring at a forkful of peas and carrots. "I mean, they can't expect us to actually *eat* this stuff.")

After school, I headed for the Johanssens', where everything seemed under control. I spent a long time playing with Carrot, and then headed over to Claudia's for our meeting. I let myself into the Kishis' at ten after five. I had arrived early on purpose, so I could talk to Kristy before the meeting. As I headed up the stairs I could hear voices coming from Claud's room.

"Hey, Stace!" said Claud, when I poked my head into her room. "You're early." She waved a handful of purple and green ribbons at me. "Look what I found in a drawer! Want me to braid a couple of these into your hair?"

"Sure," I said. "But first I just want to talk to Kristy about something." I sat down next to Claud on her bed. Kristy was in the director's chair, fiddling with a pencil.

"What's up, Stacey?" she asked.

"Well," I said, hesitantly, "I was wondering if you could make some time for me during the meeting. There's something I want to ask everyone about."

"Sure, I guess," said Kristy, giving me a curious look. I noticed that Claudia was looking inquisitive, too.

"It's no big deal," I said. Suddenly, I began to wonder if I was making too much of a few silly incidents. Would my friends think I was nuts?

I didn't have too much time to wonder, though, since just then the other members of the BSC began to arrive. Shannon showed up first, looking exhilarated, and told us her debate team had just won a big match against another school. "That gives Stoneybrook Day one of the best records in the state!" she said.

We congratulated her. "What was the debate about?" asked Claudia.

"Well, it was mainly about whether the two-party system can survive in today's United States," said Shannon. "My team's position was that it can't, because the changing political scene demands responsive — "

Claudia was nodding as if she knew what Shannon was talking about, but I had a feeling

Shannon had lost her somewhere around "mainly." What she was saying was sort of interesting, but I have to admit my attention wandered when Mary Anne came in and insisted we check out the new jacket she'd bought at the mall. Claudia and I were both happy to give our expert opinions on *that* matter.

Jessi and Mal showed up soon after, just as Kristy was preparing to call the meeting to order. They settled in quickly, since Kristy insists on starting our meetings on time.

"Order!" said Kristy, as soon as Claud's clock clicked over to five-thirty. "Let's get started," she added. "We have a lot to talk about today. For one thing, there's our holiday party. It's only a week and a half away, and we have some planning to do."

"I had a great idea for decorations," Claud began, but Kristy cut her off.

"Just a second," she said. "There's another thing we need to discuss before we start on the party."

"Oh, right," said Claud, looking at me.

"Stacey?" Kristy asked. "Did you want to talk to us?"

Suddenly I had butterflies in my stomach. For a second, I considered telling Kristy to forget the whole thing. What if my friends thought my fears were ridiculous and decided I was too immature to be a good sitter? "Maybe I — " I began, ready to drop the subject before I'd even brought it up. But I was interrupted by a ringing phone.

Kristy reached over and grabbed it. "Baby-sitters Club!" she said. "Oh, hi, Mrs. Newton." She listened for a minute and then told Mrs. Newton she'd call her back. After she hung up, she turned to Mary Anne. "Who's free next Tuesday night?" she asked. "Mrs. Newton has a meeting to go to, and she needs a sitter for Jamie and Lucy."

"Let's see," said Mary Anne, checking the record book. "It looks like either Shannon or Claud."

That job ended up going to Claud. As soon as Kristy hung up after calling Mrs. Newton back, the phone rang again — and again. Each time, I felt relieved, since every phone call meant I could put off the time when I'd have to tell everybody about my silly fears.

But you know what? When I finally had a chance to explain what was going on at the Johanssens', my friends didn't act as if I were being silly at all.

"Oooh, creepy!" said Jessi. "I wonder if there's a ghost in that house."

"A *ghost?* I don't think so," said Claud.

"What *I'm* wondering about is that so-called meter reader. I'd keep an eye out for her and her husband, if I were you."

"What was that thing about the glass again?" asked Mary Anne.

I read down the list again. These were the nine items I'd come up with the night before:

1. Carrot going wild in the house, chewing things up.
2. Carrot growling at me when I let myself in.
3. The glass in the sink.
4. The warm coffeemaker.
5. The Kleenexes in the wastebasket.
6. Carrot's leash in the wrong place.
7. The kitchen smelling like toast.
8. The incident with the meter reader.
9. The missing newspaper.

I didn't even mention the *tenth* thing: the glass in the sink again. The list seemed long enough without *that*.

"It seems like most of those things could be explained pretty easily," said Shannon. "Like the warm coffeemaker — it might be on a timer, the way you said. And Carrot's behavior might be just because he misses his family. But when you put them all together, they *are* pretty weird."

"I agree," said Kristy. "But at the same time, I'm not sure that there's any more *to* it. I mean, the house hasn't been broken into, right, Stacey?"

I shook my head. "It's not like anything's been stolen," I said. "It's just that I have this awful feeling that I'm not the only one who's been in that house during the last week."

"But how could anybody else get in if they didn't break in?" asked Claud, frowning. I could tell that she was already imagining herself as Nancy Drew. (She's read every book in that series at least twice, even though her parents would rather she read "real" literature.)

"That's the question," I said. I shook my head. "Look, it's probably all in my mind. I feel much, much better just talking about it. But there's not really anything else we can *do*, is there?"

"I guess not," said Mary Anne, looking concerned. "Just be careful over there, okay? And let us know if any more weird stuff happens."

"I will," I said. "Thanks, guys. Okay, let's talk about our party now."

We spent the rest of the meeting planning our holiday party. There was a lot to discuss, since we wanted to make sure nobody felt left out or slighted. That meant celebrating *all* the holidays: Hanukkah, Christmas, and Kwanzaa (that's an African-American holiday). We had to figure out what kind of food to have, what games to play, and what presents to pass out. Plus, Kristy was still worried about whether we'd have snow for the sleigh ride the kids were counting on. She appointed herself "Weather Watcher."

We were in the midst of planning a trip downtown to shop for little presents when the phone started ringing again and we had to stop to line up a few more jobs.

Between calls Mal mentioned that her youngest sister, Claire, had been talking a lot about that escaped prisoner. He still hadn't been caught, but as far as I knew the police thought he was probably a long way from Stoneybrook by this time. I had forgotten all about him, but it sounded as if some of our younger clients were worried. Kristy said her stepsister Karen had mentioned it, and Claud said that when she'd sat for the Kuhns the day before, all three kids talked of nothing else.

"Great," said Mary Anne, with a sigh. "I'm supposed to sit for them tonight."

"Well, if anybody can calm them down, it's you," said Claud.

"Talk to them about the party," suggested Jessi. "That should take their minds off the prisoner."

"Whatever you do, just *don't* promise them

a sleigh ride," said Kristy, laughing.

By the time our meeting broke up, I was feeling better than I had in days. Talking to my friends had definitely been the right thing to do, even though we hadn't exactly solved my mystery.

Wednesday

Wow! Claudia, you weren't kidding when you said the Kuhn kids were worried about the escaped prisoner. In fact, they are beyond worried. I would have to call them obsessed! No matter how hard I tried, I couldn't convince them to drop the subject . . .

"Hi, Mary Anne," Mrs. Kuhn said, smiling, as she answered the door that Wednesday night. "How are you? How's Logan?"

"I'm fine, and so is Logan," said Mary Anne. "I'm supposed to say hello to Jake for him."

Logan is a big favorite of Jake Kuhn's, and Mrs. Kuhn is happy about that, since she likes Logan. She wasn't happy about it at first, though. See, what happened was this: Mary Anne, who sits fairly often for the Kuhns, had noticed that Jake seemed to be missing having a man in his life. (The Kuhns are divorced, and Mr. Kuhn lives in Texas. The kids don't see him that often.) Mary Anne figured it would be good for Jake if Logan dropped by once in a while when she was sitting for the Kuhns, and she was right. Jake and Logan really hit it off. But Mary Anne was very, very wrong about something else.

What was she wrong about? Well, she had asked Logan to come over while she was baby-sitting, and she didn't clear it first with Mrs. Kuhn. Bad move, Mary Anne. Plus, she didn't talk to the rest of us in the club about her plans for one of our regular clients, which is also a no-no.

Anyway, when Mrs. Kuhn first found out about Logan's visits, she was pretty mad. The way she saw it, Mary Anne was using baby-sitting time to entertain her boyfriend. For a little while, it looked as if she might even tell other BSC clients about what had happened. Everybody in the club was worried that the BSC's reputation might be ruined, and we were all kind of ticked off at Mary Anne. (She didn't take that too well, although for the most part she managed not to cry in front of us.)

Then, finally, Jake explained to his mom that Logan was coming over to see *him*, not Mary Anne. After that, everything was okay. In fact, as I just mentioned, Logan is now a favorite of Mrs. Kuhn's, and he's welcome at the Kuhn house anytime. And Mary Anne is closer than ever to all the Kuhn kids.

"It's awfully quiet here," said Mary Anne, as Mrs. Kuhn was putting on her coat and finding her car keys. "Are all the kids home?"

Mrs. Kuhn nodded. "I told them no TV tonight, but I said they could listen to the radio while they finished up their homework. They're probably in the living room."

Once Mrs. Kuhn had left, Mary Anne went in search of the kids. She found them in the living room, huddled near the stereo cabinet, listening intently to the radio. "Hey, guys!" said Mary Anne cheerfully. "What's up?"

"Shh!" said Jake, putting his finger over his lips. "There's a bulletin coming up." He turned back to the radio, but not before Mary Anne had noticed how scared he looked. She studied Patsy's and Laurel's faces, and saw that they seemed pretty upset, too. Now, Jake is eight, and fairly mature for his age. But Laurel is six, and Patsy's only five. Mary Anne didn't like to see them frightened. She reached over their heads and snapped off the radio.

"Hey!" said Jake. "I was listening to that. They're giving important updates on the escaped prisoner."

"Such as?" Mary Anne asked.

"Such as he might have been seen in Mercer yesterday," said Jake. "That's only twenty miles away from here."

"And a lady saw him in New Hope, too," added Laurel.

"The bad guy is coming!" said Patsy, her eyes round.

"I heard those reports earlier," said Mary Anne, reaching out to give Patsy a comforting hug as she spoke. "They weren't *confirmed* sightings. And the police are all over the place watching out for this guy. I don't think it does us any good to worry."

"But — " Jake began.

"But nothing," Mary Anne said. "Your sisters are too young for this. It's scaring them." She didn't add that Jake seemed frightened, too. No need to make him defensive.

"I'm not scared!" insisted Laurel stoutly.

"Me, either," added Patsy. But she sounded less sure.

"We want to catch him!" said Jake. "If we did, we might get a reward and our pictures in the paper and everything."

"Let's leave catching him up to the police, okay?" said Mary Anne. As she spoke, she had to hide a smile. After all, the members of the BSC have been involved in a few mysteries, and we don't always leave things up to the police when we should. But, as Mary Anne told herself, we're quite a bit older than Jake and his sisters.

Mary Anne saw Jake gazing longingly at the radio, and decided to take Jessi's advice and try to distract the kids by talking about the holiday party. "Are you guys ready for the big party?" she asked. "I know my friends and I are looking forward to it."

"Me, too. It's gonna be awesome!" said Jake. "I can't wait to go flying over the snow in that sleigh."

Mary Anne sighed. "I guess you talked to the Arnold twins," she said. She knew Kristy was going to *love* hearing about this, especially since there still wasn't a single flake of snow in the forecast.

"Marilyn and Carolyn said we'll have to

dress up in our warmest clothes for the sleigh ride," said Laurel.

"I have a new snowsuit!" cried Patsy. "It's pink and purple, my favorite colors. Want to see it?" She grabbed Mary Anne's hand and pulled her toward the door.

Mary Anne looked back at the older kids and shrugged. "Be right back, I guess," she said, grinning. Then she let Patsy drag her to the hall closet. She admired the snowsuit, but refused to let Patsy wear it inside. "You'll get way too hot," she explained.

When Mary Anne and Patsy returned to the living room, guess what they found? Right. Jake and Laurel were sitting next to the radio again, listening for news about the convict. Mary Anne shook her head, frustrated, and turned off the radio one more time. Then, as Jake and Laurel sat frowning at her, she looked around, trying to come up with another distracting subject.

Her eyes lit on something Patsy had just picked up. "What's that?" she asked, pointing to the little wooden toy.

"It's a dreidel," said Patsy.

"Oh," said Mary Anne. "What do you do with it?"

"You spin it," said Jake. "It's a top."

"We play with it during Hanukkah," added Laurel.

"What do the symbols on it mean?" asked Mary Anne. "And what's Hanukkah all about, anyway?" she asked. "I always wondered. Do you get presents, like I do on Christmas?" She figured she had hit upon a topic that would be good for a few minutes, at least. She already knows about Hanukkah, of course, but she *also* knows that kids love to explain things.

"We do get presents, but it's not really like Christmas," said Laurel. "It's a smaller holiday than that. We pay more attention to lighting the menorah than to opening presents."

"The menorah's a big candleholder. We light one candle every night for eight nights," Jake explained, fully involved in the conversation now. "It's to remind us of this time long, long ago when these people thought they only had enough oil for one night's worth of light. But something wonderful happened, and the oil lasted for eight nights."

"After we light the candles, we eat the latkes and get little presents or Hanukkah gelt," said Laurel.

"Latkes?" asked Mary Anne. "Gelt?"

"Latkes are potato pancakes," said Patsy, rubbing her stomach. "Yum."

"And gelt is money, or chocolate coins wrapped in foil," said Jake. "You can use it to play the dreidel game, but then you might lose it. See?" He picked up the little top and showed it to Mary Anne. "First you each put some gelt into the 'pot.' Then you take turns spinning the dreidel. The 'symbols' are really Hebrew letters. If it lands on this letter," he went on, pointing to a figure carved into one of the four flat sides of the top, "you take nothing from the pot. And this other letter means you put something *into* the pot. But if it lands on this one," he said, pointing to a third, "you take the whole pot."

"And if it falls on that one," added Patsy, pointing to the fourth side, "you take half the pot. It's fun."

"It sounds like it," said Mary Anne. "In fact, Hanukkah in general sounds like fun."

"I made my own menorah out of construction paper this year," said Laurel. "Instead of lighting real candles, you add a yellow paper flame to one candle every night. Want to see it? It's in my room."

"Sure," said Mary Anne. Then she remembered the radio. She glanced at Jake, but he seemed busy with the dreidel. Mary Anne followed Laurel upstairs and admired the menorah, which was sporting all its "flames," since Hanukkah was already over.

As Mary Anne and Laurel came back into the living room, Mary Anne saw Jake reach out quickly to switch off the radio. He looked up at her guiltily. Patsy, who had been listening, too, seemed frightened again.

"Any news?" Mary Anne asked. She was tired of reprimanding Jake.

"Nope," Jake said, shaking his head. "Just the same old stuff." He imitated an announcer's voice. "The prisoner is still at large," he proclaimed.

Mary Anne thought for a second. Then she made a quick decision. If she couldn't divert the kids' attention, maybe it was better to focus it and channel their worries into a game. "I really think we're safe from the prisoner," she said. "But maybe it would be fun to *pretend* we're in danger. So, what if a 'bad guy' really was headed this way?" she asked. "How would we catch him? What kind of traps would we make? What would we do so he could never, ever get into the house?"

Jake grinned up at her. "I have some *great* ideas," he said. "All we need is some rope, a bucket, and an alarm clock . . ."

For the rest of the evening, the kids played "catch the bad guy." (Mary Anne kept them from getting *too* wild.) By bedtime, they were exhausted, happy, and, according to Mary Anne, worry-free. Her idea had worked, for that one night, anyway. But she knew the Kuhn kids — and many others — wouldn't *really* rest easy until the prisoner was caught.

It wasn't there.

I rubbed my eyes and looked again. How could it be? I *knew*, beyond the shadow of a doubt, that I had left my watch on the Johanssens' kitchen table the day before. I remembered taking it off before I washed out Carrot's water dish, and I remembered placing it in the middle of the table. I had put it between the salt and pepper shakers, and I had made a mental note of the place so I wouldn't forget to pick up the watch on my way out.

Of course, I had ended up forgetting it anyway. I'd left it on Wednesday afternoon, before I went to the BSC meeting. I guess I was a little distracted, thinking about how I was going to bring up my "mystery," so I walked off without my watch. I forgot all about it until the next morning, when I was getting dressed for school and realized my watch was missing.

So there I was, in the Johanssens' kitchen,

staring at the place where my watch was supposed to be. And it wasn't there. It was my favorite watch, too: a see-through Swatch with a red watchband.

I stood there gaping at the spot where my watch *wasn't*. Then, suddenly, I heard a creaking sound from directly above me. Once again, I felt those little hairs on the back of my neck stand straight up. Was somebody walking around upstairs? I spun around, looking for Carrot. He had been eating his breakfast just a second ago. Where had he *gone*? I was counting on him to protect me if there was an intruder in the house. After all, Carrot and I had bonded over the last few days. I'd walked him and stroked him and played with him and, most importantly, I'd fed him. Wouldn't it follow that he'd take my side if there were some kind of a fight?

"C-Carrot?" I called in a wavering voice.

I heard a scrabbling noise, again from directly above me. But this time my little neck-hairs just lay there calmly. I *knew* what that noise was, and I knew who was making it, too. It was Carrot himself. He must have made the creaking noise, too. Carrot likes to sleep underneath Dr. and Mr. Johanssens' bed. I guess it's just another little "cave," to him. The only problem is that, while he has no problem wiggling his way under there, he can't seem to figure out how to get back *out*. So, if you call him the way I just had, he panics and starts scrabbling around trying to squeeze himself out from under the bed. I've seen him do it, and it's a riot.

I laughed to myself, just picturing it. And as soon as I laughed, I felt much better. So what if my watch wasn't where I remembered putting it? I was probably just remembering wrong. It was nothing to get so upset about. I glanced around the kitchen, hoping to see the watch somewhere else. I could tell by the kitchen clock that I would have to leave soon if I wanted to be on time for school.

Then I saw it. My watch was lying in plain sight on the kitchen counter, next to the breadbox. I picked it up and strapped it on, shaking my head. "My memory must be playing tricks on me," I said out loud. Then I called, in a louder voice, "Later, Carrot! Be a good boy," and I let myself out.

I was ready to let the watch thing go — I really was. I blamed myself. I chalked the incident up to my bad memory. But what happened later that day had nothing to do with my bad memory.

Here's the story: On Thursday afternoon, as soon as school let out, I headed back over to the Johanssens'. It was warm out that day, warm but gray and overcast. In fact, it was drizzling a little. (Kristy had pointed out that if it were only twenty degrees colder it would be snowing.) I wasn't wearing my new coat — I'd have *roasted* in that thing. Instead, I had on this fun yellow slicker with a hood on it, like a kid's raincoat.

When I got to the Johanssens', Carrot didn't even give me a chance to take off my slicker. He wanted to go right out. He was waiting at the door with his leash in his mouth and his little tail wagging. "All right, buddy," I said, bending over to clip his leash on. "Fine with me. We'll take a nice, long walk. I hope you don't mind getting wet." Carrot pranced happily as soon as we were on the sidewalk. It was clear that he didn't mind the weather.

We walked for quite a while. It was relaxing to stroll along, feeling the misty air on my face. Carrot seemed to like it, too. Every so often he'd stop and shake himself off enthusiastically, setting his collar tags to jingling.

By the time we got back to the Johanssens', Carrot was soaked. I had a feeling he was going to be smelling pretty "doggy" for awhile, unless I dried him off. "You wait here," I told him, hitching his leash to a railing on the front porch. "I'm going to get a towel." I unlocked the door, let myself in, and kicked off my wet boots on the doormat. Then I ran upstairs to the bathroom, hoping I'd find an old towel to wipe Carrot off with.

Now, I'm not a snoop. If I were, I'd have had plenty of opportunity to poke around in the Johanssens' house. But, until that day, I hadn't even been *in* the family bathroom upstairs. There was a small one in the basement, and I'd used that one a few times, but the upstairs one seemed private, somehow, and I'd stayed out until that day.

So, anyway, I wasn't snooping. I was just looking around for towels. There were some hanging on the towel racks, but they looked too new and too white to use for drying off a sopping dog. Then I saw a small closet next to the shower. "Aha!" I said, pulling the door open. "The towels must be in h — "

I stopped in the middle of the sentence. Why? Well, it was those darn hairs on the back of my neck. They were standing at attention again. Here's what I was staring at on the shelf right at eye level: a hairbrush.

That's right, a hairbrush. And if you think there's nothing scary about that, how about if I add *this* bit of information? The hairbrush contained hairs. Bright red ones. And there isn't one single person in the Johanssen family who has red hair.

The hairs in that brush were lit from above by a light that had gone on automatically when I opened the closet. There was no mistaking their color. I stood there staring at them, and all kinds of thoughts ran through my brain. First I thought about each of the Johanssens in turn, just to make sure I wasn't forgetting that one of them was a redhead. Next, I thought about why the idea of *red* hair made me so nervous. That didn't take long to figure out. It was the escaped prisoner. Didn't he have red hair?

Then another awful thought burst in. What about that supposed meter reader? Her hair was as red as hair can be. And — and I had overheard that she might be looking for a place to live!

Those hairs on my neck were standing up straighter than ever. I grabbed a navy blue towel off the top shelf, slammed the closet door shut, and ran back downstairs. I left the towel draped over the banister while I put my boots back on. Outside on the porch, I locked the door behind me and unhooked Carrot from the railing. Then, pulling him along with me, I ran all the way over to Claud's and pounded on the front door.

"What *is* it?" Claud asked, when she came downstairs to find me (and Carrot) panting at her front door.

"Hair!" I said.

"Air?" she asked. "You need oxygen? Is that why you're breathing so hard? Should I call 911?"

I shook my head vehemently. *"Hair!"* I repeated, still trying to catch my breath.

"Hair? You're having a hair emergency? Like, a really, really bad hair day?" She looked me over. "It's a little mussed up, but it's not *that* bad," she said, grinning a little. "Really, Stace, what's the matter?"

Finally I could talk again. "I found hairs in this hairbrush at the Johanssens'," I said. Claud looked bewildered. "*Red* hairs," I finished. A light went on in her eyes.

"*Red* hairs?" she asked. "Do you know what that could mean?" Claudia's mind works fast — it's all those mysteries she's read.

I nodded.

"Let's go search the rest of the house for evidence," said Claud eagerly.

"But — " I said. My first impulse was to stay away from the house.

"But nothing," she said. "We'll have Carrot with us for protection. Anyway, you have a responsibility to the Johanssens. Let's go!"

She grabbed her jacket and we headed over to the Johanssens'. Carrot trotted along between us, looking pleased to have two humans walking him at once.

Back at the house, we began a methodical search, Claud leading the way. Carrot followed us from room to room, carrying Mister Manny-Man in his mouth.

First we checked the living room. None of the stereo equipment was missing, and the TV and VCR were both where they always were. Nothing else looked at all suspicious. Next, we went through the dining room.

"What's this?" Claud said, bending over the table. "Look! Crumbs!" She pointed.

"Um, I think *I* left those there," I said, a little guiltily. "I was eating some crackers while Carrot had his dinner yesterday." That reminded me that he was probably ready for today's dinner, so we headed into the kitchen. Claud looked around while I fixed Carrot's food.

"Looks normal in here," she said. "No mystery glasses or anything."

"Want to see the hairs?" I asked her.

"Definitely," she answered. "Lead me to them."

We headed upstairs, and Claud took a good look at the red strands. "This is *real* evidence," she said, with a gleam in her eye. She bent over for an even closer look. Just then, I heard a sound on the stairs. Claud heard it, too; I could tell by the way her body stiffened. She turned to look at me, and her eyes were wide. She put her finger over her lips, and we waited without speaking. The sound came closer. Somebody was coming up the stairs.

Claud was facing the door, and I was facing

her. I was too scared to turn around and look. But suddenly I saw her break into a huge smile. "Carrot!" she said. "I should have known it was you. How was dinner?"

I turned around to see Carrot coming toward us, wagging his tail. I could have kissed him. "I never thought I'd be so happy to see a dog," I said. That made twice in one day that I'd been frightened by Carrot. Next time I wouldn't be so jumpy.

After that little scare, the rest of our search was uneventful. Except for one thing. Down the hall from the bathroom, between the Johanssens' room and Charlotte's, there's a little table, and on that table sits a beautiful little blue glass vase. That is, there's usually a vase on the table. That day, the table was empty, and the blue glass vase — now sporting a huge crack — was on the floor beneath it.

"Oh, no!" I said, picking it up. "I guess Carrot could have broken this," I said to Claud. "And if he did, I feel sort of responsible. I'd better replace it before the Johanssens get back. I hope it's not too expensive, though. I'm already broke from Christmas shopping."

"*Maybe* Carrot did it," Claud said, frowning. "But I'm not so sure. You know what I think? I think it's time for an emergency BSC meeting. Let's call Kristy."

CHAPTER 11

By five-thirty that afternoon, there were five of us in Claudia's room. Shannon had a drama club event, and Jessi was sitting for Becca and Squirt, but the other BSC members had all made it to the emergency meeting.

Kristy was sitting, as usual, in the director's chair. "This is sounding serious," she said, tapping her pencil on Claud's desk.

"Definitely," Claudia agreed. She was sitting next to me on her bed, trying to wrestle open a bag of Starbursts. Finally she tore the cellophane with her teeth, shook out a few candies, and then passed the bag to Kristy.

"So what do we do?" asked Mary Anne, who was sitting on my other side.

"Well, for starters, I'd like to see that list again," said Mal. She was in her usual spot on the floor. "Do you have it with you, Stacey?"

"As a matter of fact, I do," I answered, pulling it out of my jacket pocket. "I don't know why, but I've been carrying it around. I never thought I'd be adding to it." I glanced down the list and shook my head. "I thought these *other* things were creepy," I said, "but they're nothing compared to those red hairs in the brush." I passed the list to Mal.

"Are you absolutely positive they were red?" asked Kristy, leaning forward and giving me an intense look.

"They were red," I said evenly. "I'm sure of it. Anyway, Claudia saw them, too." I was a little annoyed. Did Kristy think I was making this stuff up or something?

"I'm sorry, Stace. It's not that I don't believe you," said Kristy. "I'm just trying to get the facts straight. After all, if we call the police — "

"No way are we calling the police!" I said. "I would be totally embarrassed to parade into the police station carrying a hairbrush with a few red hairs in it. They'd think we were nuts, especially since the house shows no signs of being broken into."

"I think Stacey's right," said Mary Anne softly. "We're better off just working together on this." She gave the word "together" special emphasis, and underscored her meaning with a significant Look at Kristy. Mary Anne can't stand it when she feels as if people aren't getting along.

"So, back to Mary Anne's question, what do we *do*?" asked Mal. She looked down at the list. "I mean, it seems pretty obvious by now that *something* is going on over at the Johanssens'. I'd bet a month's baby-sitting earnings that you're not the only one who's been in that house, Stacey."

I gulped. Of course, that was exactly what I had been suspecting all along, but it was one thing to suspect, and another thing to hear it said straight out like that. "I don't know if anybody would take that bet, Mal," I said. "*I* sure wouldn't." I gave a little shudder. "This whole thing is really creeping me out."

"Well, there's one step we definitely have to take," said Claudia firmly. "The key thing is to make sure that Stacey isn't alone at the house anymore. One of us should always go with her when she checks on Carrot." She paused to rub my shoulder reassuringly.

"You don't have to do that," I began to protest. I didn't want any special treatment. Somehow, I still felt as if I should be able to handle the situation on my own.

"Don't be silly," Kristy said. "Claudia's right. After all, the Johanssens are due back on Sunday, right? That's only a few days away."

Mary Anne checked the record book. "It shouldn't be hard to schedule things so one of us goes with you each time, Stacey." She made some notes in pencil, frowning slightly as she worked out a schedule.

While we waited for Mary Anne to finish, we went on discussing the mystery.

"If you ever *do* see signs of somebody breaking in, that's when we should call the cops," said Kristy thoughtfully. "But I guess you guys are right. For now, I don't know what they could do that we couldn't."

"No," mused Claudia. "The only thing they might do, if they had the manpower, that is, would be to stake out the house." She had a familiar look in her eyes: the "Nancy Drew" look, I call it. It's as if her mind becomes this computer, flipping through the Girl Detective Database, pulling out all the mystery-solving possibilities. Claud may not be great in school, but she never forgets the plot of a Nancy Drew book.

"We can do that!" said Mal excitedly. "You know how you can see the Johanssens' house from Jessi's house? Maybe we could have a sleepover there this weekend. We could watch the house all night! I'll ask Jessi to check with her parents."

"Great idea," said Krisy. "I'll bring some — "

"I've got it!" Mary Anne said suddenly, interrupting Kristy. Then she looked up and blushed. "Sorry," she said to Kristy, who looked annoyed. "It's just that I have this schedule all worked out. It was a little complicated, but I think it'll work just fine." She passed the record book around. "If you guys can check to see when you're supposed to go to the Johanssens' with Stacey, I'll let the others know about their shifts."

"Good job, Mary Anne," said Kristy, looking over the schedule. Obviously, she'd forgiven Mary Anne for interrupting her. "I see I'm down for Friday afternoon. Weren't we thinking of going downtown that day to shop for presents for the party? Maybe we can meet — "

"Oh, my lord!" I burst out, interrupting Kristy again. She looked even more annoyed this time. "Sorry, Kristy," I said. "It's just that something's been nagging at me ever since Claudia mentioned the word 'key.' "

"Well? What is it?" Kristy asked, raising an eyebrow.

"You know how we keep thinking that if somebody had broken into the house we'd see signs of it?" I asked. "Well, what if they had a *key*?"

"What do you mean?" asked Claudia. "How would anybody get hold of a key?"

"There's one hidden in the Johanssens' yard," I said. Suddenly everybody was silent for a few seconds.

Then they started talking at once. "Where is it?" asked Kristy.

"Have you checked it lately?" asked Mary Anne.

"Who else knows about the key?" asked Mal.

"Whoa, whoa!" I said, holding up my hands. "Slow down. First of all, you have to swear you'll never tell anybody else if I tell you where the Johanssens keep the key."

"Of course," said Kristy. "Anyway, after all this, they may want to find a new place."

"Well," I said, "it's under this rock by the back door. I don't know of *anybody* else who knows where it is, Mal. And no, Mary Anne, I haven't checked it lately."

"Well, what are we waiting for?" asked Kristy. "Let's go over there right now and check it out."

We all looked at each other. "Why not?" I asked. "Let's go."

About ten minutes later, we were standing around the back door of the Johanssens'. I had Carrot on his leash — I'd told him he was a lucky dog, getting a bonus walk that day —

and I was about to turn over the rock.

"Wait," said Kristy. "Let's make sure nobody's walking by. We don't want anybody to guess that this is the hiding place."

Claudia went around the corner and took a good look up and down the street. "The coast is clear," she hissed on her way back into the little circle we'd made around the rock.

I handed Carrot's leash to Mal. Then I reached down and picked up the rock. Everybody gasped.

There was nothing under it. *Nothing.*

"Oh, my lord!" said Claudia. "It's gone!"

We were all speechless. But horrible images were running through my head. Images of red-haired men unlocking the Johanssens' door and slipping inside. Breaking into a house is easy, if you have a key. And there'd be no signs that you *had* broken in. No signs — except for things like water glasses in the sink. I sat down on the back stairs and put my head in my hands. Carrot sat down next to me and nudged me with his nose, as if he knew I was upset.

"Hold on, hold on," said Kristy. "Let's not panic here. There may be a perfectly good explanation for why that key is missing."

"Such as?" asked Mal, looking confused.

"Such as maybe that key is the one the Johanssens' gave Stacey," Kristy said calmly.

"Oh!" I said, instantly relieved. Kristy had to be right. "That makes so much sense. That *must* be it."

"Still, I'd feel better if we stuck to that schedule I made," said Mary Anne. She looked a little shaken.

"Definitely," said Kristy. "Stacey, I'll walk over here with you after school tomorrow, okay?"

"And I'll come over here with you in the morning," added Claud. She bent down to give Carrot a pat. "You're going to have lots of company, Carrot," she said. Carrot's ears perked up. He looked around at us and wagged his tail.

Carrot was happy about the company, and I have to admit that I was, too. On Friday morning I stopped by Claud's house on my way to the Johanssens', and it was great to have her with me as I went through my morning routine there. Nothing seemed out of place, and nothing frightening happened, but I was still glad that I wasn't alone.

In the afternoon, Kristy walked to the Johanssens' with me after school. On the way there, she talked about nothing but the weather reports. She was growing more and more nervous about whether there'd be snow in time for our sleigh ride, which was only a week and a day away. "On one channel they said there's a cold front coming, and on another channel they're predicting sleet," Kristy complained. "I listen to every single weather report and read everything I can about it in the papers, but I *still* can't tell if we're going to have snow." She frowned and kicked at a rock. "It doesn't look good, though."

"Let's just keep our fingers crossed," I said. "There's not much more we can do about it, is there?"

Once again, everything was normal at the Johanssens' that afternoon — so I was feeling much better when my friends and I headed downtown for our shopping expedition. We found terrific presents for our Christmas party, and then I cleaned out my wallet buying a vase to replace the one Carrot had broken.

After our shopping trip, we walked over to Claud's for our BSC meeting. The phone rang so much that afternoon that we didn't have a spare second to discuss the mystery, and I was just as glad. I was tired of thinking about it.

I didn't realize until I was home that night that I'd left the vase at Claudia's. But it didn't seem to matter. After all, I just had to take it over to the Johanssens' before they got home, and I still had all day on Saturday to do that.

Friday

I'll say one thing for the Pike kids: they're never predictable!

Tell me about it.

I thought we had a great idea for an afternoon activity.

It was a great idea. My brothers and sisters usually love art projects.

Well, this one didn't seem to hold their attention at all.

You're right. They're up to something, and whatever it is, it's keeping them pretty busy.

That Friday afternoon, while Kristy, Mary Anne, Claudia, and I were shopping downtown, Jessi and Mal were sitting for Mal's brothers and sisters. The two of them were pretty proud of themselves. The night before, they'd spent an hour on the phone talking about what they could do with the kids, and they'd come up with a great idea.

It's not easy to find an activity that will keep all seven of the younger Pike kids happy. After all, there's a wide spread in their ages, and they have different interests and abilities. But Mal and Jessi had hit on the perfect plan — or at least that's what they *thought*.

They had decided to have the kids make potato-print wrapping paper for the holiday party. You know, you take potatoes, slice them in half, and carve a design into the cut end. Then you dip the potato-printer you've made into poster paint and stamp it all over the paper you're decorating.

"This is great," Mal had said enthusiastically, when she and Jessi first came up with the idea. "It's an art project, which my brothers and sisters always love, and it's easy, which is good for us. The older kids can help the younger ones. And everybody will feel like they've contributed to the holiday party. It'll be messy," continued Mal. "But we'll spread newspaper all over the place, and when it's time to clean up we'll just roll it up and throw it away."

And that's exactly what Jessi and Mal were doing the next afternoon. They had set out some snacks, for when the kids got home, and then they'd turned to covering the kitchen table — and the floor and the counters — with layers and layers of newspaper.

Claire, who attends the morning kindergarten session, was the only one home so far. (Jessi and Mal had *raced* home from school in order to set things up before the other kids arrived.) Now Claire followed Mal around, pestering her with questions.

"What are we going to do?" she asked. "What's that paint for? Why can't I open the jars?"

"We'll explain everything when everybody else is here," Mal said patiently. She didn't want to describe the potato-print process more than once.

"But Mal-silly-billy-goo-goo, why is there paper everywhere?" Claire asked. Being five, she loves two things best: being silly and asking questions.

Mal decided to head her off before she got *really* silly. "The papers are to keep us from making a mess," she explained. "Claire, would you like a job?"

"Yea! A job!" said Claire, jumping up and down. "What do I do?"

"You can pick out seven really good potatoes," said Mal, showing her a basket full of potatoes that sat in the middle of the kitchen table. "Make sure you choose the best ones, okay?"

Claire looked serious, the way little kids always look when you give them a job. She nodded, rolled up her sleeves, and started to pick carefully through the potatoes. Jessi and Mal exchanged a glance and tried not to giggle.

A few minutes later, just as Mal and Jessi finished their preparations, Vanessa and Margo came bursting into the kitchen. "Hi! Hi! Hi!" Margo yelled. She's always full of energy when she comes home from school. She hugged Claire, who was still sorting potatoes. "Claire-y!" Margo said. She and Claire consider themselves best friends, and they miss each other on school days.

"School is fun but I'm glad it's done," proclaimed Vanessa, who wants to be a poet and often speaks in rhyme. "The weekend's here — let's give a cheer!"

Mal and Jessi humored her with a big "Hurray!" just as the triplets — Adam, Byron, and Jordan — and Nicky showed up.

"Hurray for what?" asked Nicky.

"For the weekend," Jessi explained.

"Oh," said Nicky. "Well, hurray! I love weekends."

"That's not all you love," said Adam, with a snicker.

"Cut it out!" cried Nicky, who had suddenly turned beet red.

"Nicky and Marilyn, sitting in a tree," Jordan chanted, under his breath.

"K-I-S — " began Byron, but Nicky whirled around and gave him a fierce look.

"Leave me alone," he said. "I *hate* girls."

"Aw, Nicky, even me?" Jessi asked, trying to lighten the mood. The triplets are always picking on Nicky, and it drives him crazy. All he wants is to be accepted as "one of the guys," but instead he just gets teased.

"I like you," Nicky said gruffly, turning to Jessi. "But you're the *only* girl I like." He scowled at his sisters.

"Okay, guys," said Mal, hoping to change the subject. "Who wants a snack before we start on our project?"

"What project?" asked Adam. "We're doing a project?"

"That's right," said Jessi. She glanced questioningly at Mal, who nodded. It was time to tell the kids what they'd be doing. "We're going to make potato-print wrapping paper for the presents we'll pass out at the holiday party."

"Yeah!" yelled Claire.

"Baby stuff," muttered Jordan.

"We thought you boys could help cut the designs," said Jessi, looking at the triplets. "The younger kids can't do that, you know."

"No problem!" said Byron, swaggering a little.

Snacktime was a little hectic, as meals usually are at the Pike household. The kids have very different tastes in food, so the kitchen is kind of a madhouse when everybody is looking for something to eat at the same time. Most of the kids were happy with the things Jessi and Mal had put out: peanut butter, crackers, bananas, and raisin bread. But Byron insisted on having salami on his peanut butter sandwich, and Claire wanted all the raisins picked out of her bread before she would even *touch* it.

Eventually, everybody had eaten and Jessi and Mal decided it was time to begin. "Okay," said Mal. "Take a seat at the table and help yourself to a potato."

"I picked them out!" interrupted Claire. "They're the best ones."

"Thank you, Claire," said Mal. "Now, you can each design two potato prints, because the first thing we'll do is cut our potatoes in half. After that, you can figure out what design you want, and one of the older kids will help you carve it. Then you can pick your colors and start printing."

Jessi was opening the paint jars and pouring paint into foil pie plates. "We have a lovely red here," she said, pretending she was one of those glamorous ladies on the TV game shows. "And a positively *delicious* green. Not to mention a divine purple and an elegant yellow." She displayed the pie plates as she spoke, and everybody cracked up. Then they set to work.

At first, Jessi and Mal exchanged congratulatory glances. Everyone was involved in the project, just as they'd hoped. There was some squabbling, but generally speaking things were going smoothly. Jessi did notice, she told us later, that Nicky and Adam, in particular, seemed very distracted. And Mal overheard Byron asking Vanessa, in a whisper, whether she'd gotten "the things."

Mal was helping Claire cut out a half-moon shape on one of her potato halves when the phone rang.

"I'll get it!" yelled Nicky, jumping up from the table. He ran past the phone in the kitchen, and answered the one on the hall table instead. Jessi and Mal couldn't hear a word of his conversation.

Five minutes later, the same scene was repeated, only it was Vanessa who jumped up to grab the phone. And a few minutes after that, Adam got up to *make* a phone call.

"What's going on here?" asked Mal.

"Nothing," said Nicky, looking innocent. Just then, the doorbell rang, and he ran to answer the door.

Jessi and Mal heard some whispering and giggling in the front hall, and then footsteps pounding down the basement stairs. Nicky reappeared a few minutes later, still trying to look as if nothing were happening. "Did somebody just come to the door?" Jessi asked him.

"Um, yes," he answered, unable to lie when questioned directly. "Just Buddy. And Matt."

"You invited two friends over without asking?" asked Mal.

"Not really," said Nicky. "I mean, I didn't exactly invite them. But can I go downstairs and play with them, as long as they're here? We have a — sort of a *project* we're working on."

"We're going, too," said Adam, as he and Byron and Jordan popped out of their seats.

"Well, I guess it's okay," said Mal. "But next time let us know beforehand if you want to have people over."

Jessi and Mal thought that was the end of it, but the "project" seemed to go on for the rest of the afternoon. The phone and doorbell kept ringing, and the Pike kids took turns disappearing into the basement. The triplets, who are old enough to be responsible, assured Mal and Jessi that they were being careful, and that the project was nothing dangerous, but they insisted that they couldn't — and wouldn't — tell what it was.

"Just what we need," Mal said to Jessi at one point when they were by themselves in the kitchen. "Another mystery."

"Right," said Jessi, pressing her potato onto the wrapping paper to create a red snowman print. "At least this one doesn't involve escaped prisoners."

She and Mal finished up the wrapping paper project on their own, sitting at the table with the paints surrounding them. They printed snowmen, wreaths, menorahs, and stars with their potatoes, trying hard to ignore the giggles wafting up from the basement. They figured they'd find out soon enough what the kids were up to, since keeping a secret is never easy in a family with eight kids!

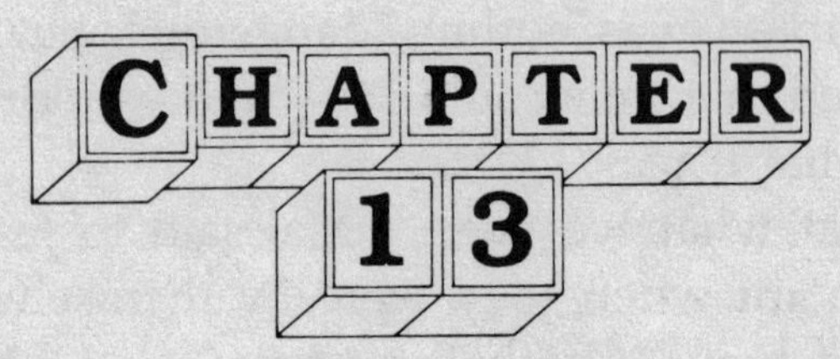

"I'm starting to think you like old Eggplant more than you like me."

"Robert! I do not. And for the thousandth time, his name's *Carrot*." I giggled into the phone. Robert was pretending to sulk because I was canceling a date we'd planned for that night, so I could sleep over at Jessi's. I knew he didn't really mind, because he'd already told me about an "awesome" basketball game he was dying to watch that night.

I hadn't told Robert anything about the mystery at the Johanssens'. Somehow, I just wanted to solve it myself — or, rather, with the help of my friends. I've never been the type to want her boyfriend to jump in and rescue her. Plus, I knew Robert would worry if he thought I might be in any kind of danger. (For that same reason, I hadn't said a word to my mom.)

Anyway, things had seemed fairly normal at the Johanssens' the last few times I'd been there. That Saturday morning, Jessi and Mal had accompanied me over there, and we hadn't noticed a thing out of place. Still, we were planning to go ahead with our sleepover/ stakeout.

While we were at the Johanssens', Jessi had come up with a wild idea for a new kind of surveillance. "Hey, we have that same phone machine at my house," she'd said, pointing at the one on the kitchen counter.

"It's easy to use, isn't it?" I said. I had been checking the machine for the Johanssens, playing any messages that came in and copying them down on a small notepad.

She nodded. "It has a lot of neat features, too," she said. Then her eyes lit up. "Hey! I just thought of something awesome. You know what this machine can do? You can call it from another phone and make it 'listen' to what's going on in your house."

"Huh?" I asked. Mal looked puzzled, too.

"It's called 'monitoring room noise,' " said Jessi. We can call here from my house tonight, punch in the machine's special code, and listen to what's going on over here."

"Whoa!" I said. Suddenly I understood what she was talking about. This would add a whole new dimension to our stakeout.

"Cool idea. But how do you find out what the code is?" Mal asked.

Jessi didn't blink an eye. Instead, she picked up the answering machine and turned it over. "It's right here," she said, pointing to a sticker. "See? The number is one-four-three. That's easy to remember. My family uses that as a code to say 'I love you.' You know, because each number represents the number of letters in those words?"

"One-four-three," I echoed. "I can't wait to try it."

That evening, Mary Anne came to the Johanssens' with me. We were loaded down with our overnight bags, since we planned to head straight to Jessi's as soon as we had finished with Carrot. I showed Mary Anne the answering machine code and told her about Jessi's idea.

"That sounds really sneaky," said Mary Anne. "Are you sure it's legal?"

"Sure, why not?" I asked. "I mean, I can come to this house anytime I want. This is just like letting my *ears* come over here, without my body showing up. What could be wrong with that?" I patted Carrot on the head. "Right, Carrot?" I asked. He pressed his nose into my hand, which I understood to mean, "Right, Stacey."

After a short visit with Carrot, Mary Anne and I headed over to Jessi's. Everybody else was already there, and they were gathered in the kitchen. Kristy was making popcorn in the microwave, Claudia and Mal were stirring up dip and putting chips into bowls, Shannon was pouring soda for everyone, and Jessi was heaping a plate with brownies she'd just taken out of the oven.

"Ahem," I said. "Is this a stakeout — or a *pig*out?" Everybody cracked up. I laughed too, and grabbed a handful of popcorn.

As soon as the food was ready, we sat down around the kitchen table to eat and plan our night.

"We're in luck," Jessi said. "In case you haven't noticed, it's nice and quiet here tonight. Becca's over at Haley's for the night, Aunt Cecelia went to a double feature, and my parents are holing up in the den with a pile of movies to watch on the VCR."

"Great," said Claudia. "That means we can spy on the Johanssens without anybody spying on *us*."

"What's our plan?" asked Mary Anne.

"Total surveillance," said Kristy, sounding like somebody in one of those action movies.

She held up a pair of binoculars. "These are Watson's. He uses them for bird-watching, and they're really high-powered."

"I brought some, too," said Mal, leaning over to rummage around in her backpack. "But I don't really know how to use them. How do you *focus* these things?"

"I'll show you," said Kristy, taking one last bite of brownie and moving over to sit next to Mal. Shannon and Mary Anne leaned over their shoulders so they could hear what Kristy was saying.

"Meanwhile, what about that phone thing?" I asked Jessi.

"We can try it anytime," she said.

"Are you sure it'll work?" Claudia asked.

"There's only one way to find out," Jessi answered with a grin. She reached for the phone. "What's the number?"

I told her, and she punched it in. Then she waited a few seconds.

I was holding my breath. What if something horrible happened? What if there *were* an intruder in the house? Suppose he happened to answer the phone. What would we *do*?

"There goes the beep," Jessi said. Quickly, she punched in a few more numbers. Then she listened intently.

"What do you hear?" I asked. "Is somebody over there?"

"Are there footsteps?" asked Claud.

Jessi shook her head, and passed the phone to Claudia, who was next to her.

"Do you hear that tinkling noise?" asked Jessi. "That's the only suspicious sound I can make out."

Claudia listened for a moment and shook her head. Then she passed the phone to me. "I hear the noise," she said to Jessi. "But I can't figure out what it is. It does sound suspicious, though. I wonder if we should hang up and call the police."

I put my hand over my right ear and pressed the left one to the phone, trying hard to hear what they were talking about. At first, I couldn't hear a thing. Then, suddenly, I heard it. I burst out laughing. "You *guys*," I said. "It's Carrot! That's the sound of his collar tags jingling while he walks around." I reached over and hung up the phone, still laughing. Claudia and Jessi looked sheepish.

Meanwhile, everyone else was clustered by the window. They were passing the binoculars back and forth and peering at the Johanssens' house.

"Whoa!" said Kristy suddenly, stepping back from the window. "Did you see *that*?"

"What? *What?*" asked Claudia. "Is somebody in there?"

Kristy looked white. "I think so," she said.

"I just saw a light go on in one of the upstairs rooms."

"I saw it, too!" said Mary Anne.

"Claud, dial the police!" cried Kristy, focusing her binoculars on the house once more. "Tell them to get right over to — what's the exact address, Stacey?"

"Hold on, hold on," I said. "Claudia, put down the phone. You guys are really jumping the gun. That light went on because it's on a timer."

Kristy put down the binoculars and looked around at me, embarrassed. "Oh," she said in a small voice.

"Hey," I said, trying to lighten things up. "Let's enjoy ourselves. We can still stake out the Johanssens', but we don't have to do it full time. We can just keep checking up with the binoculars and the phone."

"Great idea," said Claud, sitting down at the table and helping herself to another brownie. "I brought Pictionary. How about if we play while we're hanging around?"

And for the next hour or so, that's what we did. We stuffed our faces while we played, and every so often one of us would pop up to take a look at the Johanssens' through the binoculars. We also called the answering machine regularly.

By the time we finished our game (Claudia's

team won, as always, since she's the best at drawing), it was becoming obvious that nothing much was happening over at the Johanssens'. If there *had* been an intruder over there, he was definitely staying away that Saturday night. "Looks like our stakeout is a bust," I said.

Kristy, who was taking one last look out the window, suddenly gave a loud whoop.

"What is it?" I asked. Everybody rushed over to the window.

"Snow!" said Kristy. "It's *snowing*!" She did a little dance in the middle of the kitchen floor. "All *right*!" she said, pumping her fist. "I heard on the radio this morning that if we did get snow tonight that would probably mean lots more is on its way."

"So the kids might have their sleigh ride after all," said Mary Anne. "That's great."

"Hey, there's another good thing about snow," Claud said thoughtfully. "It's great for when you're tracking people. We could check for footprints around the Johanssens' now."

We thought that was a perfect idea. (I think we were happy for *any* excuse to go out in the snow and catch snowflakes on our tongues.) And at the last minute, I remembered that the vase I'd bought was over at Claud's, so we went to her house and picked it up.

It was beautiful outside, with these big soft

snowflakes swirling gently down. And since it had been a little colder for the past few days, the snow was already sticking to the ground.

Over at the Johanssens', there wasn't a track to be found. I let Carrot out for a second, and he rolled around in the snow looking perfectly thrilled to be outside. Then Claud and I headed inside to take the vase upstairs while the others waited on the front porch. We pulled off our boots, left them on the front doormat, and headed up the stairs with Carrot following behind.

"Now *that's* creepy!" Claudia said a second later.

All I could do was nod. We were standing in front of the little hall table. And sitting on top of it was — you won't believe this — a perfectly *un*cracked blue glass vase, just like the one I held in my hands.

I didn't sleep too well that night. Long after the last brownie disappeared, long after we'd finished watching the last video, I lay awake in the little sleeping bag nest I'd made on one of the Ramseys' living-room couches.

I just couldn't turn off my mind. I kept thinking about all the strange things that had happened at the Johanssens' during the last two weeks, but no matter how many times I went over the list, I couldn't make sense of it. It didn't help that the list had been topped off only hours earlier when I discovered that blue vase sitting on the hall table.

The Johanssens would be back the next day, and I knew they had no idea how happy I'd be to see them. As long as — I crossed my fingers — nothing else happened in the next few hours, they'd never have to know what I'd gone through in their absence. If there *had* been an intruder, he'd never try to get into the house once they were home. Still, I knew I should probably tell them anyway.

"Stace?" Suddenly I heard a whisper coming from the other couch. "Stacey, are you awake?"

"Uh-huh," I answered. "What's up, Claud?"

"I just keep thinking about that vase," Claudia whispered. "Promise me you won't go over there alone tomorrow morning, okay? I want to come with you."

"Sure," I said, yawning. I checked my watch. It was four A.M. Morning wasn't too far off.

I must have fallen asleep for at least a *few* minutes, because the next thing I knew, Claudia was waking me up. "Stacey," she was saying. "It's already after nine. We'd better head over to the Johanssens'."

I rushed into my clothes, and Claud and I tiptoed out the door, leaving the rest of our friends still asleep. We hurried over to the Johanssens', kicking through the fluffy snow that covered the sidewalks. "We must have gotten four inches already," said Claudia, "and it's still coming down." She stuck out her mitten to catch a snowflake.

I looked ahead as we turned the corner to the Johanssens', and saw something that made me blink and look again. "Claudia," I hissed.

"Check it out! Footprints." I pointed to the Johanssens' front walk. The snow had been kicked up, and while you couldn't see distinct treadmarks, it was obvious that someone had been into — or out of — the house.

We stepped carefully up the walk, trying to avoid disturbing the prints. (Claudia said the police might need to photograph them.) Then, as I was searching for my key, Claud gave a little snort and tapped me on the shoulder. I turned to see what had made her laugh, and there on the porch was the Johanssens' paper, neatly folded and waiting to be picked up.

I sighed. Once again I'd gotten nervous about nothing. The tracks had obviously been made by the delivery person.

"Okay," I said to Claudia. "So much for jumping to conclusions. Let's stay calm from here on in, okay? All we have to do is make it through this one last morning."

"Got it," said Claud, giving me a little salute. "Calm is the word."

We grinned at each other and I opened the front door. Carrot came trotting up to greet us, and I bent down to pat him. "Good boy, Carrot," I said, rubbing his ears. "I'll miss taking care of you." He gave me one of his patented sloppy kisses. Then he ran to find his leash.

Claud and I took Carrot on a quick walk,

first across the street and then around the block. "Do you know your family is coming home today?" Claud asked him. "Bet you can't wait to see Charlotte." Carrot wagged his tail and grinned, almost as if he understood her.

Back at the house, I mixed up Carrot's breakfast and served it to him. Then Claudia and I wandered through the house, checking one last time to make sure everything was in order for the Johanssens' return. Everything was. Including that blue vase, still sitting on its table. The one I'd bought, its twin, was over at Jessi's. I planned to return it to the store. I didn't understand how or why that other one had appeared, but I couldn't see any reason for me to waste my money replacing a vase that wasn't cracked!

Claudia and I headed back downstairs to say a final good-bye to Carrot. As I walked into the kitchen, the answering machine caught my eye and I checked to see that there were no blinking lights on it. The machine was fine, but what sat *next* to it on the counter made my heart begin to race. "Claudia!" I called, my voice cracking a little. "Come here!"

"What?" she called from the dining room, where she was straightening up the big pile of mail that was waiting for the Johanssens.

"This message pad," I said, "It's — it's not like I left it."

"What changed?" asked Claud, coming into the kitchen.

"The pages *I* wrote on have been folded back," I said. "And the new top page has a phone number written on it — in handwriting I don't recognize!"

"Are you *sure* it wasn't there before?" asked Claudia, walking over to look at the pad.

"Positive," I said. We stared at the number for a few seconds. Then I reached for the phone.

"What are you doing?" asked Claudia.

"I'm calling this number," I said calmly. That's how I felt: calm. Suddenly I had a feeling that I was going to solve the mystery after all. The phone rang four times and then, with a strange click, it was answered. I put my hand over the receiver. I wasn't sure yet what I would do when I heard the person on the other end.

As it turned out, there *was* no person. The phone was answered with a recording. I listened for a few minutes, and then I hung up.

"Claud, let's go round up the others," I said firmly. "We're going to the train station."

"What — why — ?" Claud began to ask questions, but I just grabbed her arm and pulled her toward the door. We ran back to Jessi's and found the other members of the BSC, still in their pajamas, chowing down on waffles that Mr. Ramsey had made.

"Listen, everybody," I said quickly. "How fast can you all get moving? I have this hunch . . ." I explained about the phone number on the Johanssens' message pad, and how when I'd called it, I'd heard a recording about train schedules. I told them that if we were ever going to find out who our red-headed intruder was, the time was now. "He's going to be at the station this morning," I said. "I just know it."

My friends left the table — without even finishing their waffles — and got dressed in no time. Half an hour later, we were at the train station.

Since it was a Sunday morning, there weren't too many people in the waiting room. And out by the tracks, there were only three or four little groups of people, waiting for a train from New York that was due any minute, according to the announcements being made over the loudspeakers. My friends scattered, in order to "cover" the whole station. Claudia stood next to me as I scanned the area, disappointed at not having spotted anyone with red hair.

Suddenly, I felt a jab in the ribs. "That must be him!" hissed Claud. "Back by the newspaper machines." I turned to look, and saw a man in a long, dark coat bending over a newspaper vending machine. He wasn't wearing a hat, and his hair was red. Bright, flaming red.

I stared at him as he pulled a newspaper out of the machine and straightened up. He turned suddenly, and I looked away so he wouldn't catch me staring. But he was paying no attention to me. He was looking past me, down the track at a train that was pulling into the station. He walked quickly toward the boarding area, and Claud and I followed right behind him.

"His hair is the *exact* same shade as the hair in the brush," Claudia whispered, as we hurried along. "I can't *believe* it. Where do you think he's headed? Do you think he stole anything — like papers or jewelry — from the Johanssens? He's not carrying a suitcase, so it would have to be small stuff. Maybe I should call the police before he gets away — "

Claud was looking at me, waiting for a response. But I wasn't listening to her. Instead, I was staring in horror at a scene that was unfolding in front of me. Here's what I saw: the train had pulled into the station, and almost the first people to get off were — guess who? — the Johanssens! Mr. Johanssen got off first, followed by Charlotte and Dr. Johanssen. I was shocked to see them, until I remembered the note on their fridge that gave their entire itinerary, including their arrival time back in Stoneybrook. I'd been so focused on finding the red-haired man that I'd forgotten they'd be on that morning train.

But I wasn't the *only* one watching the Johanssens get off the train. The red-headed man was making his way toward them. He moved quickly and deliberately, like a shark swimming toward its victims. I lifted my arm to wave at Dr. Johanssen, and I tried to call out to warn her. But my mouth had gone cottony-dry and my voice didn't seem to work right. What came out was just a squeak.

Then I saw Dr. Johanssen break into a big smile. At first I thought it was because she had seen me — but no. She was walking straight toward the red-headed man, holding out her arms as if she were about to hug him.

"*What?*" I said out loud. I turned to Claud, only to find that she too was staring open-mouthed at the scene. Without even realizing we were doing it, the two of us inched closer in order to hear what Dr. Johanssen and the red-headed man were saying to each other.

"Bill!" she exclaimed. "Bill Grauman. How *wonderful* to see you."

"Welcome home, Peggy," he answered. "Hey, there, Charlotte. How was your trip?" The man smiled as he greeted each of them in turn.

Claudia and I stood stock-still, just staring.

Then Dr. Johanssen caught my eye. "How nice of you to meet us, Stacey," she said. Charlotte flew over to give me a hug. "Of course, you two have met," Dr. Johanssen added, smiling at me and then at the red-haired man.

We looked blankly at each other. "I — I'm Stacey," I said, finally. "I'm the house-sitter."

The red-haired man held out his hand for a shake. "Nice to meet you. I'm Bill Grauman," he said. "The one who left you that note?"

"Note?" I echoed.

"Oh, dear," he said. "You mean you didn't get it?"

I shook my head. Then, suddenly, I remembered the piece of chewed-up paper I'd found on my second day of house-sitting. The note! Carrot had eaten it. "What did it say?" I asked curiously. I was beginning to get the picture, but I wanted to make sure I was right.

"It was just to let you know I'd be staying at the house," he said.

Charlotte was looking at each of us in turn, and her expression was bewildered.

Dr. Johanssen jumped in. "Bill's a dear old friend of ours from out of town," she explained. "He knows where we keep the key, and he knows he's welcome to use the house any time he's in the area for business."

"I had no idea you'd gone away," Bill said to her. "But it was just as well. I was coming in late each night and leaving early each morning, and I'd hardly have seen you anyway."

"So it was *you*," I said slowly, "who left the water glass in the sink and the phone number on the pad. And did you also — ?"

"Break that vase?" he asked, looking sheepish. "Yup. I admit it. I banged into it one morning as I was rushing to leave. Oh, don't worry, Peggy. I've already replaced it."

"Thanks," Dr. Johanssen said, laughing. Then she turned to me. "But Stacey, if you didn't know Bill was there, all those things must have scared you a little."

"A little," I admitted. I heard Claudia give a tiny snort.

"I'm *so* sorry," said Dr. Johanssen. "We should have warned you that Bill might turn up."

"I'm like a bad penny that way," joked Bill. "Always turning up. Now, how about some help with those bags? I bet you're eager to get home."

"Is Carrot okay?" Charlotte asked me.

"He's fine," I said. "He can't wait to see you. And *I* can't wait to hear about your trip. I'll see you soon, okay?" I gave her another little hug, said good-bye, and headed off with Claud to find our friends and report on what had happened.

"That was *so* wild!" said Claudia. "And now it's all, like, happily ever after."

She didn't know how right she was. When I got home that day, the first thing my mom told me was that the police had caught the escaped prisoner. It looked as if the BSC could finally stop concentrating on mysteries. It would be a relief to put our energy into planning our holiday party.

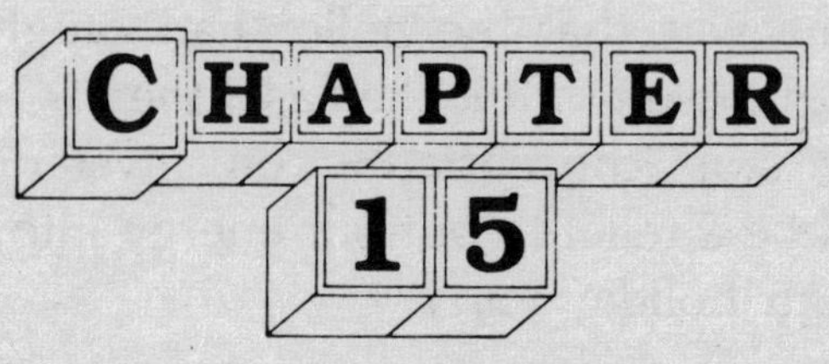

"I guess Celery must be happy to have his family back," Robert whispered into my ear.

"Robert!" I gave him a little shove. Charlotte was sitting right next to me, on my other side, and I didn't want her to hear him making fun of her dog's name.

". . . but he can't be nearly as happy as I am to have my Stacey back," Robert finished. He put his arm around me and pulled me closer.

I smiled at him and buried my chin in the big, fleecy collar of my coat. Then I glanced around at the happy faces surrounding me, and I felt totally content.

We were on our sleigh ride, and it was — well, the only word to describe it is *magical*. It was a perfect night: cold enough for us to appreciate the heavy, warm blankets that covered our laps, but not too cold. Fresh, clean white snow covered the ground, and the trees had a fluffy frosting of snow on every limb. (Yes, Kristy's wish had been granted, and there was more than enough snow for a sleigh ride.) We were skimming over the snow, pulled by two strong horses whose harnesses were strung with little bells. The sleigh I was in was actually like a big wagon, and it was *filled* with kids. So was the sleigh that followed ours. It seemed as if every single kid we had invited to our party had shown up.

Here's who was in my sleigh: me (duh!), Robert, Claudia, Shannon, and Jessi, along with Charlotte, Buddy and Suzi Barrett, Vanessa, Margo and Claire Pike, Haley and Matt Braddock, Jessi's sister Becca, and Shannon's sisters Tiffany and Maria.

In the other sleigh, along with Kristy, Mary Anne, Logan, and Mal, were the Pike boys, plus Jackie and Shea Rodowsky, Jake, Patsy, and Laurel Kuhn, Kristy's brother David Michael and her stepsiblings Karen and Andrew, Logan's sister and brother Kerry and Hunter, and Marilyn and Carolyn Arnold.

Most of our regular clients had come to the party, except for the very youngest ones. And practically every one of the kids was wearing a grin a mile wide. We'd spent the first part of the ride singing, but after we'd run through all the classics (such as "Winter Wonderland," "Jingle Bells," and "Frosty the Snowman"), we settled into a quiet mood. I leaned against Robert, patted Charlotte's hand, and smiled over at Claudia as I thought about how nice it was *not* to be worried about a mysterious red-headed intruder!

Claudia and I had talked about it while we dressed for the sleigh ride and party. (She'd come over to my house to get ready.) As we'd piled on the layers (I was wearing a silk teddy, a thermal shirt and leggings, a turtleneck, and a big multicolored sweater — I could barely move!), we had laughed about how easily all those "weird" events could now be explained.

"There's only one thing that doesn't make sense," Claudia had mused. "I understand the water glass in the sink, the warm coffeemaker, the missing newspaper, and the broken vase: those were all obviously Bill Grauman's doing. But what about Carrot's behavior? Like that day he went nuts in the house, or when he growled at you. What was *that* all about?"

"I asked Dr. Johanssen," I'd said. "She told me it was probably because Carrot doesn't know Bill that well. Having him in the house upset Carrot and made him act strangely."

Claudia had nodded. "That explains *that*," she'd said. "Now there's really only one tiny thing that's bugging me. It's about that meter reader. Was she really a meter reader? And did she ever find a place to live?"

I had laughed. "It's funny you should ask," I'd answered. "I happened to see her — and her husband — downtown yesterday. They were coming out of the electric company building, so I guess they really are employees. And they were totally lovey-dovey: holding hands, grinning at each other, *you* know. Somehow I have a feeling they made up."

"Aw," Claud had said. "Nothing like a happy ending!"

And that's how I felt that night as our sleigh whizzed along over the snow. The ride made the perfect happy ending to our mystery.

But the evening wasn't over when the sleigh ride ended. We still had a party to host.

My friends and I had put a lot of time and energy into planning the party, and, let me tell you, it was all worthwhile. The kids had a *terrific* time, and so did we.

When we arrived at Mary Anne's barn, the first thing we did was to help all those red-cheeked kids out of their outdoor clothes and give each one of them a cup of hot chocolate and a fistful of chocolate-chip cookies. (Sharon, Mary Anne's stepmother, had the hot chocolate ready for us.) As they gobbled down their food, we set everything up for the activities we'd planned.

We had decided to do a couple of things as a large group, and then break up into smaller groups for games. The first thing we did, after our snack, was to gather everyone into a big half circle for "Holiday Tales and Traditions." (That name was Kristy's idea. Pretty corny, huh? But it does describe the activity.)

First, Claudia lit a tall white candle and stood by it as she told the story of the first Christmas. As she talked, she held up gorgeous watercolors she'd done to illustrate various scenes. The kids were silent as they listened and watched intently. Next, Claudia invited Jake Kuhn up front to share the story of Hanukkah. He had brought a menorah with him, and as he spoke Claudia helped him light the candles. And finally, Claudia asked Becca Ramsey to tell about Kwanzaa, the African-American celebration that focuses on seven principles to live by. Becca brought a candleholder, too, but hers had seven candles, for the seven principles. As she explained that it was called a *kinara*, Claudia helped her light *those* candles.

The sight of that barn full of hopeful, happy children's faces lit by candlelight is not one I'll forget anytime soon.

After that, we blew out the candles and broke up into smaller groups for some rowdier fun and games. In one corner, Mal and Jessi led a group in putting together a Mad Libs version of *The Night Before Christmas*. "Okay, I need a noun, a verb, an animal, and a piece of clothing," Jessi said. Kids yelled out silly words — "Banana!" "Sneeze!" "Platypus!" "Underpants!" — and Mal wrote them all down.

In another spot, Claud and I and a group of younger kids played a version of Grandmother's Trunk, only we started with "I went on Santa's sleigh, and in my bag I carried . . ."

Shannon and Kristy had set up an area for dreidel games in another corner, and a crowd of noisy kids were trying their hands at spinning the tops.

Meanwhile, Mary Anne and Logan had slipped off quietly.

Suddenly, just as the games were winding down, there was a noisy knocking at the barn door.

"Who could *that* be?" asked Kristy loudly. "I guess I'll go see." With all the kids' eyes on her, she walked over to the door and threw it open. "Why, Santa!" she cried. "And Mrs. Claus. How nice to see you. Please, come in!"

Logan and Mary Anne, who were disguised so well with pillows, red suits, and white wigs that even *I* could hardly recognize them, walked in and set down two bulging bags. The kids swarmed around them.

"Ho, ho, ho!" Logan chortled. "This looks

like a group of *good* girls and boys. Let's see what we have for them, shall we, Mrs. Claus?"

"Certainly, dear," said Mary Anne. They opened the bags and passed out the presents as quickly as the kids could take them. Soon the room was filled with shrieks and giggles, as the kids tore open wrapping paper to find the silly little gifts we'd gotten them.

And that was the end of our holiday party, as far as *we* had planned. Logan and Mary Anne escaped during the present-opening frenzy, and came back as themselves a few minutes later, ready to help the kids get ready to go home.

But the kids had other plans.

"I have an announcement," said Nicky Pike, after climbing on a bench to get our attention. "We made a special surprise for all you baby-sitters. We've been working like elves so we could give *you* presents!"

"So *that's* what they were up to," Mal whispered to Jessi. We stood there beaming as Nicky called us up one by one to get our presents.

There was a specially decorated baseball cap for Kristy, and a snazzy pair of papier-mâché earrings for me. For Claudia there was a collection of junk food all done up in a pretty basket, and Mary Anne received a "portrait" of Tigger, drawn by Vanessa. Mary Anne also collected a gift she was instructed to send to Dawn: a pair of wild, neon-yellow sunglasses. Logan received a paperweight (a rock with his name painted on it), and Shannon was given a necklace with beads made from magazine pages. Jessi got some spangly hair ties, for putting up her hair during ballet class, and the kids had made Mal a customized sketchbook, with her name across the front in glitter.

"You guys!" said Kristy, looking as if she were about to cry. Mary Anne *was* crying. The rest of us just thanked the kids over and over. I couldn't believe how thoughtful every gift was, and how much time and energy must have gone into making all those presents. The kids we sit for are the best.

I walked Charlotte home from the party that night. We held hands (held *mittens*, really), and walked slowly, talking about the party.

Just as we reached her house, Charlotte looked up at me. "Stacey?" she said, sounding suddenly shy. "I wasn't around to help make those presents. But since you're my almost-sister, I brought you a special present from France." She handed me a tiny package.

Inside was a silvery pin with a miniature Eiffel Tower dangling from it. The word *Paris* was written across the top of the pin. "Oh, Charlotte," I said, hugging her. "This is *so* cool. Thank you, little sister!"

I gave her one last hug, said good night, and hurried home to show the pin to my mom and tell her about the evening. The pin would probably bring back some of her old memories, and I knew she would like it. I *loved* it, and I knew it would always bring back memories for me, too. Memories of a house-sitting adventure, and of a mystery with a happy ending.

About the Author

Ann M. Martin did *a lot* of baby-sitting when she was growing up in Princeton, New Jersey. She is a former editor of books for children, and was graduated from Smith College.

Ms. Martin lives in New York City with her cats, Mouse and Rosie. She likes ice cream and *I Love Lucy*; and she hates to cook.

Ann Martin's Apple Paperbacks include *Yours Turly, Shirley*; *Ten Kids, No Pets*; *With You and Without You*; *Bummer Summer*; and all the other books in the Baby-sitters Club series.

Look for #19

KRISTY AND THE MISSING FORTUNE

I sat down on the loveseat with Karen and David Michael. I opened the book and started to flip through the pages. "It's in sections," I said. "This first part is like an almanac, with all the historical stuff arranged by date."

"Hah!" said David Michael, pointing to an entry. " 'April 8, 1832: Amos Murphy's best cow has been stolen.' Guess they thought that was big news back then."

"Look at this one," I said. " 'July 2, 1826. The widow Jones reports that a neighbor's hog has destroyed her dahlias.' " I laughed. "Sounds like a crime wave."

"What's the other section?" asked Karen.

"It's a directory of people who lived in Stoneybrook then. Arranged by name."

"Look up Thomas," urged David Michael. "Maybe we have some famous ancestors."

I turned some pages, looking for the T's.

When I found them, I ran my finger down the list. Then suddenly, my finger stopped. "Whoa!" I said, looking at one of the entries.

"That's spooky," said David Michael, who had seen it, too.

"Her name's almost like yours!" said Karen, who was leaning over to read along with us.

All three of us were staring at this entry: "Christina Thomas. Born September 7, 1845. Date of death unknown. Daughter of Rachel and John Thomas (both d. 1861) of Squirelot. Disappeared January 1863, under mysterious circumstances.

"Oooh," said Karen, drawing in a breath. "She *disappeared*?"

"I wonder if she's our ancestor!" said David Michael.

Christina Thomas. Her name really was a lot like mine. A chill ran down my spine — and suddenly I had this wonderful feeling. Cabin fever? Forget about it. I had a mystery to solve.

Read all the books about Stacey in the Baby-sitters Club series by Ann M. Martin

\# 3 *The Truth About Stacey*
Stacey's different . . . and it's harder on her than anyone knows.

\# 8 *Boy-Crazy Stacey*
Who needs baby-sitting when there are boys around!

#13 *Good-bye Stacey, Good-bye*
How do you say good-bye to your very best friend?

#18 *Stacey's Mistake*
Stacey has never been so wrong in her life!

#28 *Welcome Back, Stacey!*
Stacey's moving again . . . back to Stoneybrook!

#35 *Stacey and the Mystery of Stoneybrook*
Stacey discovers a *haunted house* in Stoneybrook!

#43 *Stacey's Emergency*
The Baby-sitters are so worried. Something's wrong with Stacey.

#51 *Stacey's Ex-Best Friend*
Is Stacey's old friend Laine super mature or just a super snob?

#58 *Stacey's Choice*
Stacey's parents are both depending on her. But how can she choose between them . . . again?

#65 *Stacey's Big Crush*
Stacey's in LUV . . . with her twenty-two-year-old teacher!

#70 *Stacey and the Cheerleaders*
Stacey becomes part of the "in" crowd when she tries out for the cheerleading team.

#76 *Stacey's Lie*
When Stacey tells one lie it turns to another, then another, then another. . . .

Mysteries:

1 *Stacey and the Missing Ring*
Stacey has to find that ring — or business is over for the Baby-sitters Club!

#10 *Stacey and the Mystery Money*
Who would give Stacey counterfeit money?

#14 *Stacey and the Mystery at the Mall*
Shoplifting, burglaries — mysterious things are going on at the Washington Mall!

Portrait Collection:

Stacey's Book

THE
BABY-SITTERS
CLUB ®
Claudia
Kristy
Mallory
Stacey
Dawn
Mary Anne
Jessi